Always Sexy

The Sexy Series
Book 4

NEW YORK TIMES BESTSELLING AUTHOR

Carly Phillips

ALWAYS SEXY

She's a single mom chasing a better life.
I'm a professor trying to rebuild mine.
One kiss could destroy us both.

After a false accusation nearly ended my career, I've spent years clawing my way back. Tenure is finally within reach—proof that my reputation is clean and my past is behind me.

Then *she* walks into my classroom.

A gorgeous blonde with endless legs, sharp eyes, and a smile that makes it impossible to think straight.

Amber Davis is smart, determined… and completely off-limits.

Because she's my student.

As a single mom working toward a better future, she can't afford scandal. And after everything I've been through, one rumor could end my career for good.

But the pull between us is impossible to ignore.

One stolen kiss becomes another.

One secret becomes something deeper.

We both know the risk. If anyone finds out, it will ruin

us. But the most dangerous truth?

The rumors are real.

Formerly titled Sexy Love, *previously released as a 1001 Dark Nights novella.*

CHAPTER ONE

Amber

I INSERT THE key into the lock and open the door to my new home, a simple one-story ranch that represents a whole new life in a brand-new state.

"Surprise!"

I jerk back, startled, as I realize the most important people in my life are here to greet me.

"Uncle Landon!" My ten-year-old son, L.J., dashes past me and runs into his uncle's arms. Landon's twin, Levi, who passed away before I knew I was pregnant, was L.J.'s father.

Standing beside Landon are Tanner Grayson and Jason Dare, my son's other godparents, the men who made it possible for me to purchase this house with their generosity. When I look at these three men, who I've known for the last ten years, I see three handsome, accomplished guys who worked hard to get where they are in life. Who overcame pain and hardship and stuck together through it all, including me in their long-term, deep friendship. They are like brothers to me and uncles to my son. With their brown hair in varying shades and muscular forms, at a glance they could be brothers, although on inspection, each has their own distinctive look. They only recently found their own happily ever afters, and I am so thrilled for them all.

"Welcome home," Jason says, pulling me into a hug, then passing me to Tanner and then to Landon, who still has his arm around his nephew.

"Can I go check out the rest of the house?" L.J. asks.

I nod, looking around the still-empty space. The movers will be here later this afternoon. "Go for it."

He dashes off, the echo of his footsteps and shrieks of excitement bouncing off the walls and making me smile.

"What are you guys doing here? You're supposed to be in Manhattan." And in a little while, Landon's parents, L.J.'s grandparents, are due to arrive and take him to the city for his summer adventure, leaving me ready to start one of my own.

"We decided to surprise you. Help you unpack and move in," Landon says with a grin. He's always been easygoing, even after the tragedy that befell all of us.

They never fail to do right by me, and I smile. "You didn't have to drop everything for me. You already helped enough, lending me the money to buy this place." Something I feel guilty about already.

"*Giving* you the money," they all say at the same time.

I shoot them a glare. They all know how important it is for me to be independent just like I understand why they feel obligated to help me. Not just because Levi was Landon's twin but because all three men were there the night he died in a tragic college hazing incident when the guys were freshmen, and I was a sophomore, and they feel guilty for not being able to prevent his death.

I discovered I was pregnant while I was grieving, but the guys were always there for me. As have Landon's mom and dad, Carrie and Samuel Bennett, as well as my own parents, Lydia and John, in Florida. When I quit college, packed up, and moved home, they stepped in to help me raise my son.

"Mom, look at the size of my room!" L.J. calls to me.

Laughing, I shoot the guys a warning look and head toward the hallway leading to the two bedrooms in the house, hearing their footsteps behind me.

"Do you like it?" I ask from the doorway of the room across from my own.

"It's going to be cool. You said we could paint it blue, right?"

"Light blue," I remind him. I don't want a dark-looking tomb for my son's bedroom.

"Can I get a Spiderman Fathead?" he asks of the life-size removable wall decal he's been asking for … for what feels like forever.

"Of course—oomph."

I shove my elbow into Tanner's side as he answers without asking me.

I've been saving to buy it and have already decided the superhero will be on L.J.'s wall when he returns from his trip in a few weeks.

"We'll see," I say, ruffling his hair. I want the gift to be a surprise.

"Stop spoiling him," I mutter under my breath to the guys.

Just because they own a hugely successful night-club in Manhattan and can afford whatever they want doesn't mean I will take advantage. I already feel guilty for how much they are doing for me now, paying for this house and my classes. But I desire to make a better, more secure life for L.J., and borrowing money allows me to get my degree in education and hopefully a minor in business.

I've already been taking classes part-time at home in Florida, and I need the ability to complete my studies more quickly and obtain a job that gives me summers off for my son. The guys have offered their financial help for a while. I've just been too proud, reluctant, and scared to accept.

"I'm hungry." L.J. interrupts my thoughts and reaches for my bag, which I've yet to remove from my shoulder.

"Of course you are." I give him the oversized purse I stuffed with treats and bottles of water, enough for a growing boy to be satisfied any time he asks.

He kneels down and begins digging through the bag, settling cross-legged on the floor so he can have his snack.

I look at him and grin at how his light brown hair falls over his forehead the way his daddy's used to do. I don't need to wonder if Levi would have loved his son. He would have adored the boy who looks so much like him and, of course, his uncle Landon.

"How about I order in some sandwiches," Jason suggests, even as L.J. has already dug into some chips.

"Sounds good, man. I'm starving, too," Landon says.

"I want turkey!" L.J. looks up from where he sits on the floor. "And mayo. And a pickle. And a soda. I can have a soda, Mom, right?"

I sigh, not in the mood for a soda-or-water argument. "Sure. And say please," I remind him.

He blinks and nods. "Please!"

"Amber, what do you want?" Jason asks, his fingers hovering over the phone.

"Whatever you're getting for L.J. is fine for me, too."

While the guys stand by Jason and study the app on his phone, adding in their orders, I glance at my son, who looks up at his uncles adoringly.

I'll miss my little man while he spends a few weeks with Landon's parents traveling. He is growing up so fast but this separation is necessary. If I'm going to go back to college in the fall as well as hold down a job and raise my boy, I need to get my feet wet with summer classes while I am on my own.

I moved from my hometown in Jacksonville, Florida, to Linton, Connecticut, in order to be closer to the Bennetts, giving them a chance to bond with their grandson, and it will be equally good for L.J. to have more family around since I left my parents down south. Last year, my mom was diagnosed with late-onset multiple sclerosis, and my mother and father have their hands full taking care of my mom's increasing symptoms.

I found myself at a crossroads. I could remain in Florida, continue my job as the manager of a local clothing store, taking part-time classes and hiring babysitters for L.J. when needed, or uproot our lives entirely. I gathered my courage and opted for change.

So here we are in a small college town in Connecticut, close enough to the Bennetts that they can help out while I am in school or working, and only an hour from the guys.

Now that I've made the move, my emotions veer all over the place, from excitement over my new life to nervousness because I am starting classes in a few days.

"Mom! They're here!" L.J. is standing by the window. Turning, he runs for the front door.

"Wait for me!" I've tried to teach him not to open the door until a grown-up is with him, but I sense his excitement about seeing his grandparents. It has been a long while since their last visit in Florida.

I catch up with him as he bounces on his feet by the door and I pull it open.

"Grandma! Grandpa!" L.J. calls out, finding himself swept into their waiting arms.

From the day I discovered I was pregnant, I've been embraced by Levi's grieving parents.

"Come in!" I say to the couple who always treat me like a daughter despite the fact that I wasn't married to their son.

Carrie and Samuel walk in, each kissing me on the cheek. "I see your surprise helpers arrived?" Carrie asks with a chuckle.

"Hi, Mom, Dad," Landon says. He strides over and hugs his parents.

"We can't tell you how happy we are to have you

two nearby. I know it's a huge adjustment but it's going to be wonderful," Carrie, an attractive brunette, says, her hazel eyes glowing with happiness.

It is no wonder they have such good-looking sons, I muse.

"Of course, my wife said it best," Samuel says, also beaming with pleasure.

I am so happy to know L.J. and I aren't a burden to Landon's parents, that we are giving them something to enjoy and look forward to as well.

"We *would* like to get an early start and miss later-afternoon traffic on the way to the city," he says.

"We just ordered food. Can we add anything for you?" Jason asks.

Carrie shakes her head. "We ate before we came over. How about we wait until L.J. has his lunch and then we get going?" she asks her husband.

"Sounds like a plan," Samuel agrees.

An hour later, we've all eaten our sandwiches, caught up with each other, and it is time for the Bennetts and L.J. to get on the road.

"Mom, I'll be home later tonight. I'll see you all tomorrow. You have the key to my place, right?" Landon asks.

She nods. "I still think we could just stay in a hotel."

"Nope. There's no reason you can't stay with me. I

have the room," he says of his three-bedroom in Tribeca. He found a renovated warehouse that has been turned into an oversized apartment near Club TEN29, their place of business. "I mean, we have the space," he says with the grin he always has when mentioning Vivi, his wife.

"Okay, then. We'll see you when you get home tonight or in the morning," Samuel says.

I kneel down so I'm face-to-face with my little boy. "You're sure you're ready for this trip?"

"I can't wait to see the Empire State Building and the Statue of Liberty and eat New York City pizza with Uncle Landon!" he says with a small fist pump that has me chuckling along with holding back tears. It is going to be a long few weeks, and we've never been separated before.

But I won't dim his excitement and anticipation by expressing my anxiety or fears. He'll be fine, and knowing that, so will I. "Okay then, give me a big hug and a kiss. Then we'll get your suitcase out of my car and we'll put it in Grandma and Grandpa's SUV."

L.J. puts his skinny arms around me and hugs me tight, something I cherish because I know the time is around the corner when he won't let his mom pepper him with the kisses I do now.

"Go run to the bathroom before you get on the road," I tell him.

Standing, I face Carrie and discover the other woman staring at me with an understanding expression on her attractive face. "He'll be fine. We'll keep him so busy he won't have time to be sad or upset. And we'll have him call and FaceTime every day or whenever he wants in between."

I force a smile. "I think he's handling this much better than me," I say, managing a laugh.

"Such is a mother's lot in life. But they say if you can send your child off happily without you, you've done your job. And you're doing an exceptional one. Especially since you're doing it alone." Carrie places a hand on my cheek. "Enjoy your summer, honey. Get used to classes and working and he'll be home before you know it."

Samuel clears his throat. "Are we ready?" he asks, obviously uncomfortable with our emotional reactions.

"I'm finished!" L.J. cries, running out of the bathroom and skidding to a halt by his grandfather, grasping the man's hand.

"Perfect." I smooth a hand over my flowy top that covers my leggings. "Let's switch his bag to the back of your SUV and you can get going."

The guys clean up the sandwich wrappers on the floor and throw everything into a huge garbage bag in the kitchen.

"I'll get your bag," Landon says, following L.J. out

to the cars.

While the guys wait inside, I watch as L.J. seat belts himself and I find myself waving goodbye from the driveaway, no longer holding back tears since he can't see that I'm crying.

Tanner comes up behind me. I didn't hear him come outside, I was so focused on my son. Always the most silent of the three, he wraps an arm around me and speaks, his voice a low rumble. "He'll be fine. And so will you."

I sniff. "I know." And I hold on to the thought that a big reason for both this move and the trip is to let him learn more about his father by spending quality time with Levi's parents and his twin brother, all of whom have been so good to me over the years.

The moving van arrives a short time later, and I have no more time to dwell on missing my son. I direct the movers with the furniture, watching as they put the labeled boxes in their proper rooms and the guys get to work helping me put things away for both myself and L.J. They accomplish much more than I would have alone.

During the chaos, Carrie calls to tell me they arrived safely in Manhattan and are going out for dinner later. Knowing I have nothing to worry about, I turn my focus to my new house.

Although I still have some boxes left, I am in

much better shape than I anticipated, thanks to my friends. The guys leave, and I spend the night alone in my new house, learning the new creaks and sounds and getting used to my new normal.

The next day, I work all day on the unpacked boxes, and when dinnertime comes around faster than I expected, I decide to go into town to pick up something to eat while getting to know the area where I now live.

I consider this summer a chance to find myself again, the woman I am beyond L.J.'s mother. I missed out on learning about myself before I became a parent. I figure a return to college, the milestone that changed my life to begin with, will be the perfect way to start over.

✧　✧　✧

Shane

I PUSH MY chair back from my computer, rise to my feet and stretch, my back aching from all the hours I put in at the desk in my office. If I didn't know better, I'd never believe I went to the gym this morning to work out. But I did. Then I showered, came back here, and got into the zone on my research, losing track of time, skipping lunch and working through the afternoon. Now, almost dinner hour, my stomach is grumbling, and I am way overdue for a long walk and some food.

I stride through campus, the sight of students sporadic, as summer session doesn't lend itself to kids hanging out on the lawns and in the student union. But the Circle, a cul-de-sac with a variety of restaurants and eateries, is open year-round, and I decide to head there for dinner.

As I walk, I open my phone and skim the progress I made on the paper I'm working on. Another couple of years, and I hope to move into a tenured position, something I would have thought impossible a few years ago. Shaking my head before I go *there*, I refocus on the words on the screen, a deep dive into a paper dealing with advanced quantitative economic theory and…

I bump into someone, jolting myself and causing my phone to fall to the ground at the same time I reach out to steady whoever I crashed into. My hands wrap around soft flesh and obviously feminine arms. A floral fragrance reaches my nostrils, and I find myself breathing in for a deeper whiff of the tantalizing scent.

"I'm sorry!" the woman says as I help stabilize her before letting her go and retrieving my cell.

"My fault. I was reading on my phone." I look up

and find myself staring into arresting light blue eyes surrounded by blonde hair that has been pulled up into a messy bun on top of her head, with sexy stray strands falling around her face.

"And I was looking at the directions on my screen. I'm new to the area," she explains, biting down on her full lower lip.

"Where are you headed?" I hope she is going my way despite the fact that she is, in fact, walking in the opposite direction.

"The Circle. I'm looking for restaurants. A place to eat dinner but I think I got turned around or something. I'm not very good with maps," she says, her cheeks flushing an attractive shade of pink.

I blink and try not to look like the cat who swallowed the canary when I just got my wish. We are going to the same place.

I subtly take her in, a petite but nicely figured woman, wearing a pair of black workout leggings and a white and lavender top that drapes around her body, giving me a hint of her curves that I enjoy.

"How about you walk with me? I'm headed in that direction myself. I'm Shane, by the way."

"Amber. And that would be awesome. Left on my own, I'd probably end up on the opposite end of campus."

I chuckle. "Not everyone has a good sense of direction. So where did you move to?" I ask, making conversation.

She hesitates before answering. "A small cul-de-sac on the outskirts of the school," she says vaguely, which I understand. She doesn't know me at all, and I shouldn't have asked something so personal.

We start toward the Circle, and I point out the library and the businesses that surround the campus, consisting of large companies that tend to donate to the school. Those who live in and around the area aren't solely college employees.

"Are you meeting anyone for dinner?" I ask, surprising myself with the question.

She shakes her head.

"Want some company? I can familiarize you with the area a little," I offer.

She looks up at me as we walk. "Sure. I wouldn't know which restaurant is good, and I'd planned to sit outside and read. Company would be nice."

I am selective about dating, and for good reason. But Amber isn't a young student, she is a woman close to my own age. Besides, I justify to myself, she just moved to town, which explains why I haven't run into her before now, and I am just doing a good deed by sharing a meal and telling her where to find things in her new town.

Although she is hot as hell to look at, I am not going to do anything beyond share this one meal. Even if I am more attracted to her than any woman I've met before.

CHAPTER TWO

Amber

I HAVEN'T LOOKED twice at a man in more years than I care to remember. Oh, I dated when I could, my mom watching L.J., but anyone I went out with freaked out at the mention of my having a kid or never called me again. Lately, I've been too busy being a mom and keeping my head above water financially and emotionally to worry about meeting anyone. But I am looking now because Shane is a very attractive man.

We settle into an outside table and chairs with hamburgers and French fries in front of us. I take a sip of my soda, aware of his heated gaze on the purse of my lips around the straw. We certainly share an immediate attraction, I think, dropping my stare to the food in front of me.

I don't have to look at him to be aware of his handsome face covered by a scruff of beard, warm brown eyes, and what look like soft, kissable lips. I squirm in my seat, unaccustomed to my body's reaction to the man. Any man. It has been so long since my sex pulsed in delicious response to the opposite sex.

Have I used my battery-operated boyfriend? For sure. But even those moments are few and far between with a little boy in the house. But this man with his nice body, his short-sleeve tee shirt pulling tight over his muscular frame, has me thinking about doing other things in my bed. Adult things I haven't experienced in far too long.

"So the campus is a circle with roads situated like spikes that lead to different areas and buildings," he says.

His statement brings me out of my surprisingly sensual musings, and I meet his gaze, doing my best not to blush. I hope.

As he describes the town, I am drawn by the rasp of his husky voice. "You turned down the wrong street the first time," he says, an amused tilt to his lips.

Clearing my throat, I nod. "Picking the wrong street would explain things. I've also been a little distracted."

And I'm not just talking about being preoccupied right now with thoughts of him. And my vibrator. *Oh, good God*, I think to myself. *Just stop! Focus.*

Forcing my mind back to the mundane, I go on to explain. "The movers just dropped the boxes off that need to be unpacked, and my son left to spend a few weeks with his grandparents. I'm not used to being without him." Glancing up at him, I meet his curious gaze.

"You have a son?" He blinks, and I realize he has long, thick lashes, the kind I have to use mascara to obtain.

"I do." Maybe I'm testing him, tossing this bit of information out when we are just having a friendly dinner. But I'd rather know than find myself interested in the man only to discover he is just like every guy I've dated before him. Not that I am dating him. Oh, my God, this man has me so internally flustered.

Still, my son not only comes first, he is everything in my world, and any man in my orbit needs to know it. "He's ten, and he's a great kid," I can't help but add with a grin.

"Are you married?" Shane asks bluntly, his gaze scanning my fingers, no doubt in search of a wedding ring or telltale tan line.

I shake my head.

"Divorced, then?"

I don't mind the questions. I opened the door, and of course he is curious, but people do tend to judge me. There were the moms at the preschool, where I was the youngest one dropping off my little boy, which happens when you get pregnant at the age of twenty. They stared and whispered as if I did something wrong.

I pull my bottom lip between my teeth, catching the way I nearly succumbed to awkwardness at the truth of my life. Instead I square my shoulders and own who I am. "No. I'm a single mom."

His eyes open wide. "Kudos to you. My mom raised me alone, and I know how hard it must be for you. Forgive me for saying so, but you must have had him when you were young."

"I did," I murmur and take a bite of my burger instead of explaining further. My life is complicated, my past painful, and I'm not going to elaborate with a stranger.

He leans in closer, and I catch a hint of delicious-smelling aftershave. "I didn't mean to strike a nerve."

"You didn't." I begin to shake my head and decide to tell the truth. "Well, maybe you did. People can be judgmental. But clearly, you're not, so we're good. Now can you tell me more about the shopping around here?"

His gaze settles on mine for a long moment before acknowledging my subject change with a nod of his head. "There's an Acme on the west side of campus, and if you go farther into town, there's a Stop & Shop. For the rush things you might need, there's a store on campus that sells everything from college gear to quick snacks and basic toiletries. And for real shopping, you get on 95 and head south to the mall." He follows up that summary by picking up his drink and taking a long sip.

I grab my cell and type shorthand information about everything he said into my note app. "Well, that helps. A lot. Thank you."

"You're welcome."

We eat, finishing up the remainder of our meals in companionable silence until my phone buzzes, and I glance down.

Carrie's text shows on my screen. *Shower time. L.J. will FaceTime you in about thirty minutes.*

I glance at Shane. "I need to get going. My son is going to FaceTime with me soon, and I don't want to miss the call."

"I get it. You're a good mom." He smiles at me, the beauty in his expression taking my breath away.

"Thank you. I try to be."

Because we ordered and brought our trays outside, I start to gather things together.

"I've got it," he insists.

"Okay … well, thank you for getting me to the right place. And for dinner." He paid despite my protests.

"You're welcome."

A pause ensues, the first truly awkward silent moment since we met. I don't know what to say, and he seems equally uncertain. Will he ask to see me again? Take my number? I realize we haven't even exchanged last names.

And I'm not even sure if I want to get involved with a man now. Although my best friend from Tampa, Layla, insists it's time I try dating again, I'm not ready. Considering I just moved to a new state, a new guy is the last thing I think I need.

And since Shane, despite the occasional intense and lingering looks my way, doesn't seem inclined to make a move, I decide to wrap things up. "Well, thanks again, and it was nice meeting you."

Feeling like a dork, I wave a hand in the air, turn, and walk away, hoping I am headed in the right direction this time. And doing my best not to turn around and look back to see if he is watching me.

✦　✦　✦

Shane

I WATCH THE sexy sway of Amber's hips as she walks away, damning myself for letting her go without exchanging numbers. Despite the fact that I know it is for the best. With the summer session beginning, I have two months to work on my paper in between teaching Intro to Economics as a substitute for a fellow professor, a friend who is on sabbatical.

I always throw myself into my work, determined to be successful in a way my father told me I'd never be.

My father, and I use the term loosely, is a lawyer at a major Boston law firm, who divorced my mother when I was five years old and married the partner's daughter in the firm where he worked, starting a new life and a new family. Leaving my mother to raise me essentially on her own.

Sure, there was alimony and child support, but my mom was a single parent, there for me when I was sick, picking me up after school, attending every major event in my life when my father didn't.

Yet despite being a mostly absentee parent, Zachary Warden, a top corporate attorney, expected his only son to follow in his footsteps if I wanted him to pay for college. My decision to become a college professor was a disappointment to Zachary, one he never let me forget. Not even when I graduated summa cum laude from Yale with an MBA and a minor in economics. And my father didn't pay for my education.

Instead, I took loans and worked my way through college, determined to live life on my own terms, preferring to bury myself in academia rather than legal briefs or corporate mergers. I enjoy teaching students and watching them succeed. Earning tenure will be the final step I need to ensure the future I'm working toward.

Succeeding is important to me and not to prove something to my old man, with whom I have no relationship to speak of. I have a goal, and I'm determined to reach it. Tenure and job security mean everything to me, and I nearly had my dreams derailed thanks to a student who reported me for coming on to her when I was an adjunct professor at another school.

Not only hadn't I made a pass at her, she approached me in my office, practically stripping before I could stop her. I turned her down. Not only because of the no-student-teacher-fraternization policy, but because I had no interest in the younger girl. Even after I was proven innocent thanks to another student, who did the right thing and told the truth about her friend's retaliatory behavior, the incident left a bad taste in my mouth for how my fellow professors treated me during the scandal. They ostracized me until I was exonerated. I don't need colleagues like that.

Seeking a new start, I came to Linton when a friend here told me of a job opening, and I don't regret the move. Though I date on occasion—I am a normal man, after all—I am always careful to choose women who aren't involved with the school. Women who are busy with their own careers and aren't looking for a man who would shower them with attention. I don't have much time to give. Still, it's been awhile since I've been with anyone, my paper and my teaching taking up all of my time.

Hell, I haven't thought of a woman *that* way … until bumping into Amber. And as I watch her go, I can't help but be filled with regret for letting her leave without any way of getting in touch with her again.

✧   ✧   ✧

Amber

I WAKE UP, my stomach a jumble of nerves, as I ready myself for my first college class in ten years. I dress in jeans and a pair of sandals, a silk sleeveless top with decorative roses completing the outfit. Drawing a deep breath, I eat my oatmeal and down much-needed caffeine before walking over to my backpack, where I recheck that I have everything I need.

Instead of the used laptop my mother could barely afford like I had the first time, I now pack the top-of-the-line laptop the guys in New York bought me and insisted I can't return, along with a notebook because I am still a handwritten note taker at heart, pens … and courage. I need a big heap of that.

I spent the weekend unpacking the most necessary boxes and trying to start making this new house my home, beginning with pictures of L.J. and his dad, along with those of Landon, Tyler, and Jason holding L.J. as a baby. My mind often goes to the man with whom I shared a meal and the new feelings he inspired.

Those enlightening sensations in my body have me thinking that maybe Layla is right and I should use my time alone this summer to put my toe back into the dating pool. I don't think I'm ready for the new world of online apps and swipe right or left, but a man I meet the old-fashioned way? While walking on campus?

I wished I'd had the courage to ask for Shane's phone number. Maybe if I run into him again I'll suggest we go for pizza. My treat this time.

As I am about to walk out the door, my phone chimes, indicating my FaceTime is trying to reach me. I pull the phone from my bag and answer, happy to see L.J.'s smiling face.

"Hi, Mom!"

"Hi, sweetie! How are you?" I ask, picking up my keys from the counter and swinging my pack over one shoulder.

"I'm good! I just wanted to wish you good luck. Grandma reminded me you had your first class today."

I laugh as I step out into the heat of the summer morning and lock up behind me, keeping my eye on my son's face. "What are you up to today?"

Glancing down the street, I follow the directions I looked up this morning, more certain I have the right way this time.

"We're going to the Empire State Building!" He lets out a loud cheer, and I laugh.

Samuel calls for him from another room.

"Gotta go, Mom."

"Bye, honey. Love you."

"Love you, too!" He disconnects us, and the screen goes blank.

I rush along the path to my classroom, and as I come closer, I look around and am forced to accept the one thing I avoided thinking about while going through the enrollment process and making the choice to return to school. That I am significantly older than everyone around me.

Now, as I take in the girls in their cropped tops and tight denim shorts, frayed at the edges, I come face-to-face with reality. I am out of place and don't belong here. Making friends will be nearly impossible. Swallowing over the lump in my throat, I push any negative thoughts aside. I am here to create a better life for myself and my son, not make friends my own age.

Today's class is an intro to economics, something I need for the business minor I desire. Unfortunately I struggle with math classes and don't expect even the most basic to be simple or easy.

I arrive at the classroom and walk inside the big lecture hall. Despite the fact that it is summer session, an intro class obviously pulls in a large number of students. I choose a seat in the middle, not too far up front but not in the way back, either. People fill up the seats around me.

Reaching into my backpack, I pull out my notebook and pen. I'll take out my computer if I feel the need later on. I can sense the minute the professor walks into the room because a hush descends, and the chatter stops.

I open to a fresh page and glance at the front of the room just as the professor strides up to the podium, freezing at the sight of Shane standing in front of the classroom. I never looked at my professors' names, knowing they won't mean anything to me. And in the rush of moving in and unpacking, I hadn't had time to pay attention to little details.

Hands on the podium, he clears his throat and begins to introduce himself. It never dawned on me that he might be a professor at the school, although it probably should have. To me, he was a hot guy I met on my walk to get dinner.

I glance up, taking in his professor look and demeanor. He is more serious and buttoned up than he was the other night, wearing a white collared shirt and a dark sport jacket over a pair of dress slacks. He appeals to me on a visceral level, looking sexy yet smart, his hair combed neatly back, his expression serious as his gaze scans the class.

I realize the moment he recognizes me, his eyes opening wide. I hesitate, then raise my hand in a small wave only to have him school his features into one of bland disinterest. My stomach twists in embarrassment, and I lower my arm and study the blank page in front of me.

Thanks to the wash of humiliation, I find it hard to pay attention at first, and by the time I recover, he's asking questions and calling on students.

Too late, I realize there was an assignment, and if I logged on and checked my emails, I would have known. Already behind, I fidget in my chair and try to keep up. But as he goes over the basic definition of economic theory, *opportunity cost is the value of the next highest value substitute use of that resource*, I know I'm in trouble. Math confuses me. This completely bewilders me.

I swallow hard and pray he doesn't call on me. He'd been jumping around on his class list, not going alphabetically, and at some point, I'll be up. Another five minutes drag by, with me scribbling down notes I don't understand.

"What is the definition of microeconomics?" he

asks. "Ms. Davis?"

I glance up and slowly raise my hand to let him know where I'm sitting. Although he might have already guessed by my first name if there are no other Ambers in the room.

"Umm … I'm not sure. I didn't realize there was an assignment for the first day." My cheeks flame with mortification.

He narrows his gaze. "Microeconomics focuses on how individual consumers and firms make decisions, such as how they respond to changes in price. Now, this class might be an introductory one, but it isn't a joke. If anyone thinks otherwise, you can visit the registrar and drop the course." After that reprimand, which I take as aimed at me, he moves on to other items on his agenda to discuss for today.

Upset with how my first day went and embarrassed that I come across as uncaring and disrespectful to my professor—to Shane—I can't wait for the class to end. Of course, the minutes drag, until finally he ends the session.

"The syllabus and my office hours are in the email I sent," he reminds us, his gaze landing briefly on mine. "See you on Wednesday."

I swallow hard and collect my things, aware of the rustle of noise around me as the other students do the same and rush out of the room.

I wonder if I owe him an apology or explanation or if I should just show up better prepared next time. Not that the subject matter will lend itself toward me understanding it easily.

Lost in thought, I zip up my backpack and rise to my feet, stepping into the aisle and bumping into…

"Shane. I mean Professor Warden." I stumble over how to greet him. "I wasn't watching where I was going. Again."

"It seems to be a theme," he says, his voice a low rumble.

I glance around the room, noting we are alone. "I haven't been to class in ten years. I just moved here from Florida this weekend, and I sent my son off with his grandparents for the first time. I should have checked my emails. I thought I was prepared and I wasn't. Math really isn't my thing, and this is all confusing but it won't happen again," I say, knowing I am rambling, repeating things he already knows about me in my rush to make him understand.

"Amber, relax." His hand comes to rest on my shoulder, and I feel the heat straight through to my core. My gaze flies to his, and I catch the flare of heat in his chocolate eyes before he removes his hand and banks the fire so quickly I think I imagined it.

I breathe in deep and inhale the now familiar scent of his cologne, which strikes a chord inside me and makes me even more aware of him as a man and not the teacher in charge of my class.

"It's a difficult class. You can always drop it now and take it in August when you've had more time to settle in," he says.

I shake my head, refusing to back down from something just because it's challenging. "I can do it … or are you trying to get me out of your class?"

The idea dawns on me and won't let go. As awkward as I feel, maybe he is equally uncomfortable. Because he enjoyed having dinner with me, too?

Meeting his gaze, I wait for his reply.

✦　✦　✦

Shane

I KNOW I was an ass, first ignoring her wave, then calling on her when I knew she was as thrown as I was by finding out I'm the professor of her class. The look of shock on her face said it all. In my attempt to convince myself I could handle having her as a student, I was harder on her than I normally would be on day one.

"No, I'm not trying to get rid of you," I semi-lie. No doubt it will be easier for me if I don't have to look into those pretty blue eyes every day or hide my obvious attraction to her behind the podium. "I just thought maybe, given everything going on in your life at the moment, postponing a difficult class might be in your best interest."

She straightens her shoulders, and my gaze is drawn to the swell of her breasts beneath her colorful top.

"No. I made a mistake but it won't happen again."

"Okay," I say, admiring her determination. "We'll see if you can handle the work."

She tips her head to the side, taking a step closer to me. So close I inhale her citrusy scent and my cock grows hard.

"Just like we'll see if you can handle having me in your class." She pins me with a knowing gaze, clearly having decided she has me off-kilter.

She is right.

I blow out a long breath. If I have second thoughts about not getting her phone number, those ended the minute I laid eyes on her in my classroom. Ironically, I now have access to her phone via my students' information list.

"I just thought we could get a slice of pizza or something. Get to know each other better." Those blue eyes study me with definite interest.

Interest I reciprocate, and I swallow hard, tempted beyond belief to take her up on her offer. But the past, propriety, and common sense prevent me from acting on what I want. No way will I have a relationship with a student. Not even one obviously close to my own age.

"This can't happen, Miss Davis," I tell her, my tone firm, using her last name to put much-needed distance between us.

She stares at me as if trying to decipher what was going on inside my head, pursing her delectable lips in thought.

"I don't think I'm imagining the chemistry between us," she says. "But that *Miss Davis* comment explains everything. Student-teacher. Forbidden. Got it." She lifts her backpack higher on her back. "I'll see you on Wednesday, Professor."

She turns away and walks out of the room, my gaze on her ass as she leaves.

Biting back a curse, I head back to the front to gather my things, hating how I was forced to go against every gut instinct I possess by ignoring our attraction. I want to get to know her better. I am curious about how she came to be a mother so young, wonder what happened to her baby's father, if he is still in her life, and why she decided to go back to school now.

Basically I want to discover everything about her, and that includes learning the curves of her body that she tries so hard to hide with her flowing clothing. My hands itch to slide beneath her colorful top and run along her bare skin. I am dying to close the space between us when we are alone and seal my lips over hers and find out if she tastes as delicious as I think she will.

For a man who never wanted more from a woman than a good time, who never got serious about anyone he dated, the desire I feel for all things about Amber shocks me.

Why the hell does it have to be the one woman I can't have in any manner, shape, or form?

CHAPTER THREE

Amber

OVER THE NEXT couple of weeks, determined to conquer my economics class, I pull myself together and work hard on every assignment, quiz, test, and question posed by *Professor Warden*. I do my best to put the idea of dating him out of my mind and focus on my studies. Neither one is going the way I hoped.

I can't stop thinking of him as Shane, the sexy man with whom I shared dinner … and the guy I want to kiss. I even gathered my courage and put myself out there with him, only to be shot down. Surprisingly, I wasn't hurt by the rejection, because I really do believe his being my teacher is behind his unwillingness to date me. I still give myself credit for making the overture.

Levi was the last man I truly was interested in sexually as well as emotionally. When I was a young woman, he was the love of my life. It was only as I grew up that I realized we hadn't shared enough for that to be true. I didn't know him as well as I wish I could have if he was given more time in this world. I was young, and sex had been new and exciting, but I was hardly experienced.

And the men who came after? The select few I went to bed with before they discovered I come with child baggage and run for the hills? Those men didn't exactly let me explore my sexuality all that much. The attraction I felt for my past flings wasn't the kind of instant, sizzling, all-consuming desire I feel for Shane Warden.

I have a feeling going to bed with him would be an out-of-this-world experience. I only wish I could find out if my imagination lives up to reality. I want that so badly I am willing to overlook the fact that I had a baby and my body isn't the thin, lithe one I had when I was in college the first time.

As I realize my mind has drifted back to Shane the man once more, I acknowledge I really am not doing a good job of putting him in the professor box. But if I am going to accomplish my mission, earn my degree, make my son proud, and provide him with the best life I possibly can, I have no choice but to focus on my studies. I need to at least pass my Intro to Economics class, and I am struggling. Badly.

But I have an exam tomorrow I need to pass, so after FaceTiming with L.J., who is having a blast in the

Big Apple, catching up with Carrie and Samuel, and then having my weekly check-in with each of the guys in New York, I make myself a cup of coffee and settle in to study.

✧   ✧   ✧

Shane

I SIT IN my family room, grading the most recent test I gave to the class, and groan when I come to Amber's exam. No matter how I look at it, she is one point short of passing. Although for most students, I'd chalk it up to a bad exam result, upload the grade, and move on, I pore over her test, trying to figure out what the issue is so I can help her, because she really is trying hard to succeed.

She is doing the work, reading the assignments, participating in class, and asking all the right questions when she has a problem. Clearly, she is eager to learn and is doing everything she can … on her own. Either her study techniques are an issue or the subject matter just doesn't make sense in her brain. Not everyone excels in every course, but if she really needs this as a prerequisite, she has to pass the class.

I notice, too, that she's joined a study group, which is a positive step, except that group includes a student,

Dan Markham, I had before in a math class. Dan doesn't struggle in the class the way Amber does, but he is averaging a B- and he isn't happy. In my past with Dan, the boy has issues with any grade less than an A and has a tendency to blame the teacher and not accept responsibility himself. Not that Amber would know that. It isn't my place to say anything to her, either. I hoped that Dan and the others would be able to help Amber, that they could all help each other, but that doesn't seem to be the case.

I'll have to talk to her about her grade after class today. Without a significant change, she is at risk of failing the entire course, and there is no way she can pass the final. With the right help, however, there is still hope. Although I tell myself I'd go to this extreme for any of my students, in my heart, I know I am digging deeper because this is Amber … and I feel a connection to her even if I have kept my distance.

I stand at the front of the room, trying to concentrate on the subject matter, which I know inside and out, or on the other kids in the room, but my gaze always comes to rest on Amber. Yes, she is older than the others, but she is persistent, and I admire her diligence. She sits and types in her notes, occasionally resorting to a notepad and pen, always paying attention.

I know when she is frustrated by the cute crinkle

of her nose and realize when she catches on to a concept by the bright light in those striking blue eyes. While taking exams, she twirls her hair around her finger, pulling her bottom lip between her teeth while trying to figure out the answer. And when she is antsy, she crosses and uncrosses her legs, nice long legs I admire, even when covered by jeans or leggings.

I have it bad for her, and it isn't easy to focus on what matters most. All my students. My job. Tenure.

Fuck.

I don't sleep well that night and arrive at class just in time to start the lecture. I wait until the last five minutes to hand back the exams, not meeting Amber's gaze as I slide the paper onto her desk.

After striding back to the front of the room, I turn to look across it. "You can reach me in my office if you have any questions," I say, then remind them of my office hours. "That's it for today." I pause, then say, "Miss Davis, would you stay after for a moment?"

Everyone scrambles to grab their things and leave the room. Only then do I allow myself to look at Amber and catch the sheen of frustrated tears in her eyes thanks to that test result.

Amber

GREAT. SO NOT only do I have another failing grade but now I have to face Shane in my humiliation, I think. I swallow past the lump in my throat, wondering not for the first time since starting this class if I made a mistake in coming back to school. Maybe I am too old. Maybe the subject matter is just too much for me. If I can't handle it now, when I have no other responsibilities at home, what am I going to do when L.J. comes home and demands most of my time?

I have no one to talk to, either. The Bennetts, my mom, the guys are all cheering me on and believe in me. Even L.J. told me this morning how proud he is of me. I smile at the thought of my little man. I miss him so much, but he is having the summer of his life, and I know I made the right decision starting school alone and letting him spend time with his family.

I told Layla I was struggling in economics, but my friend's joking answer was to ask my hot professor for *extra help*, and that just isn't happening. Shane made it clear he is off-limits to me. But now he wants to talk, probably to suggest I drop the course, even now, so late in the semester. The room has emptied out, and I hear the sound of footsteps coming up the aisle.

Looking up, I glance into his concerned gaze. I still have a hard time thinking of him as *Professor Warden*.

He strides over to me and settles into the closest chair, shocking me when he places his hand over mine.

"Hey."

Sparks fly at the simple touch, my entire body alighting with sudden life and need. I don't have to wonder if he feels the energy between us, too. He rips his hand away from me so fast my head spins, and he is right to do so. I can't allow myself to focus on sexual tension when I have this failing grade glaring at me from my desk. But the scent of his cologne surrounds me, mocking my attempt to keep things purely innocent and professional.

"Amber?" he asks, his voice gruff with what I think is the same desire pulsing inside of me. "What can I do to help?"

I shake my head. "I don't know. I'm doing everything I can, but nothing is enough."

"How are your other classes going?"

I blink back my earlier tears. "Fine. Good, actually." The realization helps center me. "It's just this one that's giving me fits."

Understanding lights his expression. "So it's not school that's hard for you, it's economics."

I grimace. "Right. And I wanted to minor in business, so I need this intro class for any course that comes after it."

"What about a tutor? Maybe some one-on-one instruction will help," he says.

"Are you offering?" The words are out before I can censor them.

A heightened flush hits his cheeks, and even that hint of color is sexy. I can imagine the same ruddy hue on his cheeks when we are in the middle of a hot make-out session, or when he is deep inside me while in my big, lonely bed.

He opens his mouth to reply, and I speak first. "I was kidding," I say before he can reprimand me again. "Can you recommend someone to tutor me?"

He nods. "Let me ask around, see who's available in the summer, and I'll get you a couple of names."

Gratitude rushes through me. "Thank you. I don't want to quit, but I know I can't do this on my own." And though he can't offer his own help, he came up with a solution I hadn't thought of myself. "I appreciate the suggestion."

He smiles. "I'm glad you like it. Now let's hope it works."

We rise at the same time, and I take a step back, unsteady on my feet. He reaches out a hand to steady me, pulling me forward, and suddenly I am in his arms, my head tilted backward, his mouth millimeters from mine.

"Dammit," he mutters gruffly, and as if unable to hold back from kissing me any longer, he closes the distance and seals his lips over mine.

I've dreamed of this moment many times in the last few weeks, but reality supersedes fantasy. He wraps me in his body heat as his tongue sweeps into my waiting mouth. I moan and lean into him, my long-dormant senses coming alive with the sensations he awakens inside me.

Our tongues touch, tangle, and delve deep. Gripping his shoulders in my hands, I lift myself onto my toes so I can get closer. He tastes like the mints I saw him pop during class, a fresh hint along with his unique masculine flavor, and I can't get enough.

I want more, more of his taste, more of his scent, more of him. He wraps an arm around my waist, hauling me against him, my hips grinding against his, my sex coming into direct contact with the hardness of his erection. He is big and thick, and my body softens, desire pulsing through me. I knew I wanted him. I hadn't known how much until now.

A loud creaking noise sounds, followed by the slam of the lecture hall doors.

I glance around but nobody enters the room.

"Shit." He pushes me away as if I were toxic and steps back into the aisle. "Shit," he repeats, running a hand through his hair. "This shouldn't have happened."

"But it did." And I can't say I regret it.

"It can't happen." Panic laces his voice. "Never again."

I narrow my gaze, knowing I didn't mistake the desire between us or the fact that it was mutual. "Why not?"

"For so many reasons, but the main one is that I'm your professor."

"Is it against school rules for a student to get involved with a teacher?" I ask.

His brow wrinkles adorably. "Not in writing. Although many schools do have things spelled out, not all do. However, I cannot allow for any hint of impropriety to taint my professional reputation. Been there, done that," he mutters under his breath but loud enough for me to hear.

"Can you explain?" I want to know everything about him, and if he's dealt with any kind of scandal, that will help me understand his reticence to get involved with me now.

He groans. "At my last university, a student claimed we had an affair. In reality, she was pissed I'd turned down her advances and decided to get back at me. Damn near ruined my career." He paces up and down the aisle as he speaks. "I realize we're the same age; however, there are so many issues with what's happening between us I couldn't begin to name them all. But I can't afford anyone to think I'm giving you special treatment, using my position of authority to push you into a sexual relationship… Dammit!" The pacing continues.

"So you admit there's something between us?" I ask hopefully.

He spins to face me, a scowl etching his features. "That's what you took from my concerns?"

A hint of a smile lifts my lips. I can't help it. I'm excited he feels something for me. "No," I say softly. "I understand it all, and for that reason, I'll stay away … until class ends." Then I want to get to know him.

He already knows I have a son and isn't running away because of L.J. Which means he is a good guy, something I already figured out. So I want to see if we can form some kind of relationship, as hard as it will be to find time to see one another once my son comes home.

He raises an eyebrow, obviously surprised by my easy acquiescence.

"What's the catch?"

I laugh. "The catch is I want to get to know you in another way."

"What's that?"

"The old-fashioned way. You can talk to me at night on the phone. You can text me. I want to see if we have things in common besides"—I gesture between our lips. "—"that."

Somehow I've left him speechless.

"Please let me know about a tutor as soon as possible," I say, my tone somber.

"I will."

"And *Professor Warden*? You have my number."

CHAPTER FOUR

Shane

DESPITE THE OPENING Amber gave me, I keep my distance. I was burned too badly once before by a nonexistent relationship with a student to indulge in any sort of real one. No matter how drawn I am to the bubbly blonde.

And in the last few weeks, I've seen a more radiant side to Amber's personality as she grows more comfortable both in my class and with the material. I know from Professor Anne Slater, who is tutoring Amber, that she is grasping the material thanks to the individual attention dedicated to the subject. She also has made some friends in class, her study group, which shows me the lighter side she keeps hidden beneath the busy mom or harried student. I often see her laughing, revealing a more carefree side I wish I could get to know better.

Every time I catch a glance of her smile, my dick reacts. *Remember that kiss?* it seems to ask me. *Don't you want a repeat?*

I frown and refocus on the papers in front of me, but the information blurs, and when my cell rings, I am grateful for the reprieve.

"Hello?" I ask without really looking at the number.

"Shane? It's Margo. Your step—I mean, it's Zachary's wife." She was clearly about to say *stepmother*, a term I've never been open to or welcomed.

Still, she tries. She's never been the stereotypical bitch I expected, just the second wife my father left his family for. It is hard to welcome her, especially when my own father hasn't bothered much with me and yet has been such a stubborn ass when it comes to how I choose to live my life.

"Hello, Margo. How can I help you?" I ask, my standard answer for her rare phone calls. And they are rare.

"It's your father. He … he had a heart attack," she says, her voice cracking.

Despite our fractured relationship, panic runs through my veins. "Is he … is he okay?"

"He is. The doctors are optimistic, though they want to run a few tests."

Relief flows through me. After all, the man is an ass, but he is the only father I have.

"But he's asking for you," Margo says. "Can you come visit? Tomorrow would be best because they are running tests today."

I run a hand over my eyes and groan. "I'll be there." I don't have class in the morning, and they are only located an hour away. But why in the hell does my father want to see me?

And how do I feel about it? My father either leaves me to my own devices or steps in when he doesn't approve of my choices. He's never once asked to see me for no apparent reason. True, a brush with mortality could spark a man's deepest fears, but I don't see my father reaching that deep into his soul, and apologies aren't in his vocabulary.

"Thank you. I'll let Zachary know. I'll text you the hospital information and I'll see you tomorrow," she says before disconnecting the call.

I open a beer and walk to the kitchen window above the sink and look out over my lawn. The neighbors are sitting on their deck, a drawback to this house as there are no trees as a barrier giving me privacy.

Deciding not to go outside, I sit down on the sofa in the family room, take a sip of my drink, and stare into the empty room. I need someone to talk to, someone I think will understand my past and mixed emotions about visiting my sick father. There is no way I'd burden my mother with this news, and I haven't made any friends here close enough to unload this kind of crap on.

Which leaves the only person I really want to see anyway. The same woman I've been avoiding unless I see her in my classroom. The one I've steadfastly refused to text or call despite the open invitation for me to do so.

I want to talk to Amber.

✧ ✧ ✧

Amber

SOON AFTER MY conversation—and kiss—with Shane, though I'm not thinking about that now—I received an email with two tutor names and nothing else written in the note. Ignoring the pang of disappointment that he isn't going to discuss anything personal, I jumped on the opportunity, texting both tutors and setting up a meeting with a female assistant professor who replied to me first. Knowing I have a plan sets my mind at ease about the class. I feel certain with one-on-one help I can get up to speed enough to pass and put Intro to Economics behind me.

Unfortunately I can't do the same for Shane or that kiss. I've been reliving the moment while awake and daydreaming and in my sleep at night. But he's made his intentions or lack thereof clear, and I am not going to chase after a man who isn't interested in me. I understand his reasons for not wanting a public relationship, but I offered him a way to get to know each other without anyone else being aware. And he hasn't acted on it. So I throw myself into my schoolwork.

Thanks to the tutoring, over time, my grades slowly inch up. I'll never be an economist, but I am going to get more than a D in this class. I consider a C a major accomplishment. When Shane hands back quizzes and assignments with my better grades, I see the gleam of approval in his gaze and the pleased expression on his face. He still doesn't get in touch with me the way I hoped, and after a few weeks go by, I come to accept that he is going to keep his distance and I need to respect his wishes.

In between studying, I finish unpacking my house, finish decorating L.J.'s room, and have fallen into a comfortable routine, speaking to L.J. every evening and texting with him in the mornings before I go to school on the days I have class. I also join a study group and meet with them twice a week, and though the information I learn there didn't help before tutoring, once I have a grasp on the material, I feel more comfortable contributing and gaining information there.

Because of the difficulty I have in economics, I put

aside the idea of getting a part-time job until the fall, when I know I'll be more comfortable with the classwork and be able to dedicate work hours when needed. All in all, things are going well.

I've just finished dinner and put my dishes in the sink when my doorbell rings. I wipe my hand on a dishtowel, place it on the counter, and go to answer it.

A glance through the curtains shocks me. "Shane!" I open the door, and he brushes past me and steps inside, the scent of his cologne immediately surrounding me.

"What are you doing here?" I ask.

He winces at the question. "Abusing every privilege and right I have to your personal information by showing up on your doorstep because … I need you."

At the admission, which seems reluctantly pulled from him, my pulse skips a beat. "What's going on?" I shut the door behind him.

"My father had a heart attack," he says, and when I really look at him, the pain etching his features becomes obvious.

"Shane, I'm sorry." I reach out and place my hand in his. "But I'm not sure why you need *me*?"

Of course I feel bad that his father has a health issue, but what does that have to do with me?

His intent gaze bores into mine, and I sense something has definitely shifted.

"Why do I need you? Because I haven't been able to get you out of my head since the day we met. Because I watch you from the front of the class and have to pretend I'm not completely turned on by every move you make. Because I want to know every little thing that makes you tick and then learn some more. And because when I got the call about my father and thought about who I wanted to share my deepest pain with, only you came to mind."

I draw a startled breath, completely taken off guard by his honest admission. "But … when you didn't call or text, when you ignored me except for calling on me in class, I thought you weren't interested in me that way."

A wry yet sexy smile lifts his lips. "I'm a damn good faker when I need to be. So there's just one thing I need to know for now."

My heart beats out a rapid rhythm inside my chest. "What's that?"

"Do you still want me the same way?"

I don't need to think about my answer. "I do."

Although everything that concerned him before still stands between us, he is here now, and I have no problem acting on my feelings. I move toward him at the same time he lifts me into his embrace, wrapping my arms around his neck at the same moment his lips come down hard on mine.

Pausing mid-step, he allows us the time to kiss, to drop the barriers and pretenses that held us apart, and lets us come together now. His words have stripped the defenses I built, thinking he doesn't want me. I am open to anything he desires from me now. This is my summer of new beginnings and explorations, and where better to start than with the man who desires me as much as I do him?

Threading his fingers through my hair, he tugs on the long strands, my head tilting, giving him complete access to my mouth. His tongue slides inside, and he takes control, gliding his lips over mine, nipping at my bottom lip and sucking on my tongue until my sex pulses with unfulfilled need.

"Bedroom?" he asks.

"At the end of the hall." He carries me through the house and steps inside, making his way to the bed and easing me down onto the mattress.

Standing over me, he hooks his fingers into the waistband of my leggings and pulls them down, taking my panties along with them. Eyes darkened, he studies me for a long while until I squirm under his intent gaze. Then he lifts the edges of my top and slides it over my head, leaving me in just a bra, my bottom half bared to him completely. My cheeks burn with discomfort, concern about the shape of my body rising to the surface.

"What's wrong?" he asks, obviously noticing the sudden stiffening of my muscles. He strokes a hand down my cheek. "You're beautiful and—"

"I'm not," I blurt out. "I have a stomach and stretch marks. I had a baby. I'm not anything like the women I'm sure you're used to." I bite down on my bottom lip and meet his gaze, my entire body trembling with a combination of embarrassment and worry that I ruined everything between us with my sudden burst of insecurity.

"Shh." He slides one finger from my throat to my sternum, his gaze hot on mine. "I'm not interested in any other women. There hasn't been anyone in a long while, and the only person who has my attention is you."

"But—"

"But nothing. I already know you've had a baby and I don't care. All I see are your beautiful curves." He traces the scalloped edge of my bra, dipping his finger beneath the lace and tweaking my nipple with his fingers.

I moan and my thighs spread almost of their own volition, wanting him to touch me *there*, too.

"That's it," he murmurs. "Trust me to make you feel good." He flicks his fingers in the front clasp and my bra slides down my arms. And he tosses the garment aside.

Before my brain can come back online and worry some more, he bends his head and pulls a distended nipple into his mouth, and I see stars behind my eyes and delicious sensations travel straight to my sex. Dampness settles between my thighs, and a warm pulsing feeling arouses me even more. He plays with my breasts, first one then the other, giving them equal attention and making sure to stimulate me to the point where I am squirming on the bed, my hips gyrating, reaching to fill the desperate ache he inspires.

He kisses me, swirling his tongue around and around mine at the same time he eases one finger inside me. I moan at the feeling, my inner walls clasping around him, and though it has been a long time for me, I know I can take more. I need more.

"I want you, Shane."

"And you're going to have me." He bends one of my legs, placing my foot on the mattress, and then the other, exposing me to him completely. Pumping one finger in and out, he adds a second, and I arch my hips in an attempt to pull him deeper into me.

He drops to his knees, removes his fingers, and suddenly his mouth is on my sex, his tongue gliding up and down, eating at me with a gusto that surprises me. In my brief experiences, no man has ever been that eager to go down on me before. Did they do it? Sure, but did they spend the amount of time Shane does, licking, sucking, and nipping at my sensitive flesh? God, no. And I love every second.

Building, pulsing sensation pools between my thighs, and I am so close I can almost reach the climax I so desperately want. I rub my sex against his mouth, and he chuckles, the sound vibrating into me as he begins to lick my clit, then nip at the tight bud. Suddenly I soar, the orgasm just out of reach slamming into me like a freight train.

"Shane," I moan, moving my hips back and forth against his greedy mouth until the glorious waves of pleasure subside, my legs collapse, and I fall back against the bed, my body still tingling.

The next thing I know, I hear the sound of him ripping into a condom. Levering myself up on my elbows, I realize he's stripped off his clothes and is naked, amazing in his bare masculinity. He is well built and sexy, a pleased look on his face, his mouth glistening with my juices, and my sex pulses as I realize that fact.

A glance at his thick cock, and I have a moment's hesitation, wondering if I can take him, and then his hands are on my thighs and his heavy erection poised at my entrance.

His dark brown gaze meets mine as he eases into me, starting slow, then, finding me wet, he thrusts all the way home.

"Shane." His name seems to be the only word I am capable of uttering because I feel him everywhere inside me.

"Hold on, beautiful."

I blink back tears at the endearment because I haven't been this close to a man … ever. Sexually, I have been, but what I already feel with Shane is more than the brief encounters I had after Levi. I don't know how or why I can feel so much so soon, considering we don't know each other well, but he obviously cares about my emotions and concerns. He is trying to make me feel desirable, and I do.

I so do.

And when he begins to move inside me, his serious gaze never leaving mine, my world shifts. He pumps his hips, his thick cock thrusting deep and pulling out again, my nerve endings feeling like sensitive live wires. Even though I already came once, from the throbbing awareness in my body, I could definitely climax again.

"I want you to come with me," he says, as if reading my mind.

I blink up at him, his gruff tone an indication of how close he already is. He slides a finger over my clit, and I respond with a drawn-out moan.

"Again," I urge him. "Don't stop."

He presses down and works his finger in circles, all

the while pumping into me. I feel the waves, and before I can process what is happening, I fly. I come hard, my entire being his to master as he continues to work my clit through my orgasm, lightening his touch as I come down from the high.

And then he thrusts harder and deeper, again and again. Sweat drips down the side of his face, his expression taut as he comes on a long, drawn-out groan of complete satisfaction.

✧   ✧   ✧

Shane

MY LEGS SHAKE, and I barely refrain from collapsing onto Amber's sexy body. I manage to hold myself up as I return to reality and glance down at the woman I just—well, I hadn't fucked her. And I wonder if I know her well enough to have made love to her. Either way, something monumental occurred between us.

"Can we use your shower?" I ask.

She nods, her eyes heavy-lidded, as I help her to a sitting position and, once again, lift her into my arms.

I enjoy carrying her, I think, as I slide her to her feet in the pretty white bathroom.

She pulls towels out of a small linen closet behind

the door, and I turn on the shower. Together we step into the walk-in and rinse each other off with a citrusy soap that smells like Amber. I am going to smell like her, I muse, and I'll have to shower in the morning before going to visit my father.

Something I do not want to think about.

"So tell me about your dad," she says as she pours soap onto her hands and begins soaping me up from my ankles up, a wicked gleam in her eyes as she spends a prolonged period of time re-arousing my cock.

It doesn't take long, either. But instead of staying there so we can play, she pins me with her gaze as her slick hands run up my sides. "You mentioned your mom was a single mother, too, but you never said anything about your dad."

I groan, knowing I'll have to tell her. That I wanted to confide in her all along. "My father left us when I was five. He'd been having an affair with the partner's daughter in the law firm where he worked. Ultimately, he married her, and they had two daughters."

Amber winces. "I'm sorry."

I am long accustomed to that source of hurt. "As for my mom? She was and is great. An amazing mom who did everything herself. The only good thing I'll say about my father was that he didn't shirk his financial responsibilities to us. He wasn't there for me at all, but he paid child support and alimony. We didn't want for anything. But…"

She maneuvers me under the water so the stream can rinse off the soap, and when I am clean, I begin to wash her, already accepting the fact that this isn't going to be about sex. I soap up her legs, moving my hands up her calves, knees, and thighs, letting out a grunt when I slide my hands over her sex but keep going because I know she wants to talk and get to know me.

"But?" Amber pushes, proving me right, although her eyes flared when my fingers slid over her pussy.

"But when it came to college, he'd only agree to pay if I went to law school like he did."

She narrows her gaze. "Seriously? Why did he even care if he had nothing to do with you for most of your life?" She sounds indignant on my behalf, and I appreciate the show of support.

I roll my shoulders because I never figured my father out. "Beats me. Because he likes control is the best I can come up with. Anyway, I told him to keep his money, took loans, and put myself through school." I soap up her breasts, her arms and then place her under the steady stream.

"Where?" she asks.

"Yale."

Her eyes open wide. "He should be proud. What an ass," she mutters.

"Yeah. But he's still my father, he had a heart attack, and he's asking for me."

"Are you going?" Amber asks.

"I am." I'm not feeling a sense of duty as much as the pull of a child to my parent.

She nods in understanding, then quickly washes and conditions her hair before shutting off the water.

We dry off and then, wrapped in towels, make our way back to bed. I could leave, but I don't want to go, so I climb in beside her and pull her against me.

She sighs and snuggles against me, and of course, my cock begins to perk up again. But I am well aware of the fact that just because we had sex doesn't mean I know her as well as I want to. I am drawn to her, though, and for now I am going with that.

"What about you? Tell me how you ended up a young, single mom."

✧　✧　✧

Amber

I KNOW IT is only fair I talk about myself. "I was a sophomore in college, dating a freshman named Levi Bennett, and I guess it happened. Looking back, we weren't as careful as we should have been." I bite down on my lower lip.

"Where is he now?" Shane asks.

I draw in a difficult breath. Despite how many years have passed, it is never easy to recall what happened to L.J.'s dad, and I dread the day when I have to explain the circumstances to my son.

"He died in a hazing incident at school. To hear his twin and best friends tell it, the night was brutal. He suffered a lot, and so did they. But I didn't know I was pregnant. I didn't find out until a few weeks after he died, and though I was in the middle of grieving, I knew I wanted to keep Levi's baby." I lean back into the hard body behind me, taking comfort in the wrap of his arms around me.

"You loved him."

I manage a smile, if only for myself. "As much as I was capable of at that age. And I was lucky. My parents accepted my circumstances and let me come home. They helped me raise L.J. And he has Levi's parents and his twin brother, and two godfathers."

"He's a lucky boy," Shane says.

I nod. "His uncles, real and pseudo, they feel responsible because they were there that night. They offered to pay for my school and this house, and though I said no for a while, I finally realized if I didn't take this step and leave Florida, I wasn't doing justice to L.J. or the life he deserved. The guys have been great, although I really hope to pay them back one day."

"What's your relationship with his *uncles*?" he asks, a hint of what sounds like jealousy in his tone.

"They're like my brothers."

He exhales a long breath, the rush of warm air hitting my shoulder. Then he slides his hand around and cups my breast in his palm.

Next thing I know, he's flipped me over, reaches for his jeans to grab a condom, and slides into me, making me feel utterly owned as he takes me for a hard ride.

Early the next morning, Shane wakes me with a kiss. "I've got to get going."

I roll my head to the side. "Are you going to be okay alone?"

"Are you offering to come with me if I'm not?"

I chuckle. "Funny."

He stares into my eyes as he speaks. "I'm not kidding. Want to take an hour's ride? I could use the company as well as the support."

I sit up, pulling the covers with me. "You're serious."

He nods.

"Okay, then. No class today. Study group doesn't need me. I can call in sick. Sure. I'd be happy to come," I say, and I wonder what I am getting myself into.

CHAPTER FIVE

Shane

O N THE DRIVE to the hospital, Amber and I talk more about our childhoods, how she managed raising L.J., and I learn a lot about her son.

According to Amber, he is a sweet boy with a good disposition, easy to get along with, hates baths, showers, and anything to do with water. On the plus side of that, he is a good listener, so she merely has to remind him and nudge him a time or two to get him to clean up at night. He likes superheroes and baseball. He also loves to read and is ahead of his grade. His favorite books are *Harry Potter*, and he is looking forward to making new friends in school this year.

I hope to meet her son soon, which is saying something, considering I never thought I'd be interested in a woman long-term, never mind getting to know her child.

Now I am focused on my immediate concern, dealing with my father. I stride into the hospital with Amber by my side, following the directions Margo texted to me, walking down the hall where my father's room should be located.

From a distance, I see my dad, Margo next to him, slowly making his way toward us, my father's hand on an IV pole as he walks.

"Incoming," I say, gripping Amber's hand, and she glances up at me.

"That's your father?" she asks.

I nod.

We meet up with the other couple in the middle of the hall. In his hospital gown and slippers, his face pale, expression drawn, my dad looks much older than his years. Margo, too, looks exhausted, her dark hair pulled back, no makeup, as if she's been at the hospital since my father was brought in.

"Shane! Margo said she'd called and you were coming, but I wasn't actually sure," my father says.

"I'm here. Hello, Margo." I tip my head at my stepmother, the awkwardness between all of us a tangible thing. "Dad, Margo, this is Amber. Amber, my father, Zachary, and his wife," I say stiffly.

"It's nice to meet you," Amber murmurs.

"Same." Margo smiles at Amber, her entire demeanor welcoming, while I can feel my father studying Amber, assessing her.

"Zach, you should get back to your room. The nurse said a short walk," Margo reminds him.

"Sure. Son, walk with me," my dad commands.

"If you could point out the waiting room?" Amber asks before I can comment. "I'll grab a cup of coffee if there is one."

"I'll show you," Margo says. "I'd like a cup myself. I'll be right back," she assures her husband.

Amber sends me a reassuring smile, and though it grates, I stay with my father, not wanting to upset him while he is in the hospital.

We slowly head back to my father's room in silence, and I wait until he resettles himself in bed before walking over and speaking.

"So you're okay?" I ask.

"I haven't gotten yesterday's test results back yet but I think so. It's just going to be a lifestyle adjustment." My father shifts in the bed, getting more comfortable.

"So no more steaks and whiskey?" I pull up a chair and sit down.

"Bite your tongue." My father's mulish expression is typical.

"Well, I'm sure things will have to change, and Margo will make sure you're here for a while."

A long while, hopefully, because my father isn't old at all. He just turned sixty last year. Margo threw a party. I made sure I was too busy to attend.

"So who's the woman you brought with you?" my

father asks before I have a chance to delve into why he wanted to see me.

Smiling at the mention of Amber, I glance at my father. "A good friend." I have no intention of involving a man who couldn't care less about me most days of the year in my private life.

My father narrows his gaze. "Tell me about her."

I shrug. Talking about Amber isn't a hardship. "She's smart, going back to school to make a better life for herself and her son."

"Seriously? You can do better than a single mother looking for someone to take care of her."

I blink, any hope I harbored deep down that this heart attack softened my father gone in the second it took for that shit to spew from his mouth.

"First, I said we were friends."

"And I saw the grin on your face the minute I mentioned her."

I push myself to a standing position. "Okay, I came because Margo said you asked for me, but if you're going to be your usual pompous, arrogant self, I'm out of here."

Insulting Amber is off the table. I admire all she's done with her life in the face of difficult circumstances. I am falling hard for her, and though I have to hide it publicly for now, I'm not letting her go. Especially not because my father doesn't approve. I can't give less of a shit what my father thinks.

"Wait." My dad pauses, then adds, "Please."

Folding my arms across my chest, I meet my father's gaze.

"Why did you want to see me?"

My father's expression falters, and suddenly he looks more … humble, if I had to pick a word. "When I had the heart attack, I was lying waiting for the ambulance and a lot of my mistakes flashed in front of my eyes. Things I'd done wrong, especially with you."

I'm not exactly shocked my father had a revelation when he was scared and thought he might die. But how he reacted to Amber? The man hasn't changed. I wait for Zachary to talk more before I pass full judgment.

"I wasn't a present father."

"To put it mildly."

A muscle ticks in my father's jaw. "I wanted a fresh start, and I thought if I threw money at your mother, I was doing right enough by you. I was wrong."

I swallow hard. "I'm grateful Mom didn't have it harder than she already did, raising me alone. But you were wrong. A boy misses having a father."

Something Amber's son will surely go through, I suddenly realize, my heart hurting for the little boy. Although she said he has a solid support system, uncles, grandparents. That ought to help. And if he meets and likes me, I could be there for him, too. A more local, present male influence. Once again, I am shocked that I, who never thought I had the time for anything more than my work and my future goals, am thinking about Amber and her son as more than just a summer fling.

"Shane. Are you listening? I said I know, and I'm sorry," Zachary says.

"But you still have your opinions. And those don't jibe with the way I live my life. What you said about Amber is just one example. You don't even know her, and you found her lacking and assumed she'd be using me."

My father nods. "You're right. But you don't expect a zebra to change its stripes overnight, do you?" He tries to make a joke of it, but I'm not laughing.

Frowning, I shake my head. "No. But I can't say it's going to be easy to have a relationship after all these years."

"I'm just asking if we can try."

I'm not about to argue or upset the man who just had a heart attack. As much as I resent my father, a small part of me, the little boy who missed a father at his ball games and graduations, wants more than one birthday phone call a year with him.

"We can try," I agree.

Just then, a knock sounds on the door, and Margo walks into the room. "Okay if I stay?"

"Sure, honey. Come in," Zachary says.

Margo walks over to the bed and sits on the edge. "Did you two have a good talk?"

I nod. "We did."

"I spent some time with Amber. She's a sweetheart," Margo says.

With a grin, I can't help but agree. One thing my father is right about: I can't help my reaction at the mention of Amber. She has me wanting things I hadn't imagined in my future before I bumped into her on campus.

Now all I have to do is get through the end of the summer semester, and we are free to explore what can really be between us.

✧ ✧ ✧

Amber

I SENSE SHANE'S need to think on the ride home from the hospital, and I allow him the silence he needs. If he wants to talk, I am here to listen. He surprises me when he pulls off at an unfamiliar exit.

"Where are we going?" I ask him.

"I think we need a nice late lunch, don't you?"

My stomach rumbles at his suggestion. "Yes, as you can hear." I pat my belly and laugh.

"I know of a place off this exit. A colleague mentioned it at a faculty meeting. We're here. We might as well give it a try."

I nod in agreement. "Sounds good to me. What kind of food?"

"American. Burgers, chicken, that sort of thing. I think they also have an outdoor terrace where we can eat if you don't think it's too hot."

"I'd love to sit outside."

"Good." He doesn't speak again as he drives to the restaurant.

I glance at his still-serious profile. He is clearly up-tight about whatever happened with his dad. I have to admit the man wasn't friendly to me, but I chalked it up to illness. Margo was sweet, and I enjoyed the few minutes I spent with her, although I understand why Shane has his issues with his father's wife. My parents have a happy marriage, and I can't imagine what he lived through as a child.

After a short drive off the exit, he pulls into the lot. A large framed building with a wraparound porch sits behind it. Shane helps me out of the car and leads the way up three steps to the hostess stand.

On our request, we are seated outside in a private corner where no one is around us. We each order a glass of iced tea and study the menu and place our orders, a Niçoise salad for me, a grilled chicken sandwich for Shane.

Finally, I can't take the silence any longer. "Are you okay?"

He braces his arms on the table and meets my gaze. "It's hard admitting my father's an asshole. Always was, always will be. Yes, he had an epiphany and knows he didn't do right by me, but it hasn't changed who he is deep down. And that's tough to swallow."

I reach across the table and put my hand in his. "I'm really sorry."

"Thank you." He nods, stroking his thumb over my skin. "The thing is, I'd made my peace with who he is. I just hated having it thrown in my face again."

I bite down on my lower lip. "Do you want to talk about it?" I offer.

He answers with an abrupt shake of his head. "It's fine. I'll eat a good lunch with fabulous company and put it behind me."

His more relaxed grin puts me at ease. "Sounds like a good plan to me."

I pick up my drink to take a sip just as my phone chimes, and I recognize the sound. "Sorry, it's L.J. on FaceTime." I hate to ever not accept my son's call.

"Take it," he says. "And maybe you could introduce me? As your friend?"

He sounds eager to meet my son, and a warm feeling wraps around my heart. I hit the accept button and my little boy's face shows on the screen.

"Mom! We went to the Statue of Liberty!"

I grin at his excitement. "That's so cool. Did you see the whole city?"

"It was amazing."

"Are you going to the beach this weekend?" Carrie and Samuel have been taking him to the Hamptons on the weekends to a house they rented for the summer, and during the week, they are staying with Landon and touring Manhattan.

"Probably. I hope my friend Andrew is there. He's from a place called Long Island."

"That sounds great, honey." I glance across the table at Shane, my heart in my throat.

I've never had reason to introduce a man I am seeing to my son. For one thing, I've been careful before bringing someone into his life who would only disappear a few weeks or months later, and for another, no man has been that interested.

Swallowing hard, I gesture for Shane to sit in the chair beside me. "Speaking of friends, I want you to meet a friend of mine. This is Shane Warden, honey. I met him this summer." No reason to explain to my ten-year-old that Shane is my professor.

I turn the phone so Shane can see my brown-haired little boy. "Hi, L.J. I'm Shane. Your mom has told me so much about you."

He lifts his hand in a shy wave.

"Say hi to Mr. Warden, honey. I mean, Professor Warden."

"Shane is fine. I hear you're having fun with your grandparents in New York."

L.J. nods. "Next week we're going to a Yankee game!"

Shane grins. "I also heard you love baseball. Maybe we could play some catch when you get home. I could dust off my catching mitt."

An excited light hits my son's brown eyes. "That would be awesome!"

"I'll look forward to it. Here's your mom." He fully turns the phone back to me.

I have to fight back the lump in my throat and the tears forming in my eyes. This man, he's barreled into my life or I've barreled into his and turned my world upside down. He makes me feel things long forgotten, and now he is including my son.

I swallow hard. "Hi, honey. I need to go. I'm sitting in a restaurant." At least no one is around us, or I wouldn't have taken the call and disturbed other guests' lunch.

"Okay. I love you, Mom."

"Love you, too, baby."

"I'm not—"

"You'll always be my baby," I say before he can finish. Laughing, I say goodbye again and we each disconnect the call.

I draw a deep breath and meet Shane's warm gaze.

"Well, that went well," he says.

"It did." Acting on impulse, I lean forward and kiss him, expressing everything he makes me feel without using my words.

His tongue slides against mine, the moment quickly heating up, the kiss going on, arousal settling low in my belly, desire pulsing between my thighs.

He places a hand on my leg and breaks the kiss, his dark eyes meeting hers. "We really need to get back to your place."

"We so do."

He straightens in his seat. "But there's something we need to talk about first."

With my mind still hazy from his warm lips on mine, I'm not thinking all that clearly. "What is it?"

"Where we go from here. At least for the next two weeks while class is still in session."

I freeze, knowing the wonderful feelings I've experienced since he showed up on my doorstep are about to disappear. Temporarily, I hope, but it hurts. Still, I am adult enough to understand and handle it.

I straighten my shoulders. "I get it. We can't be seen together." But is he going to disappear from my life as if our time together never happened? "What are you thinking?" It is his job on the line. No matter how my heart feels, because I know I am falling hard for him in a very short time, I can handle a few weeks apart. I have to.

"I need every possible angle of professionalism covered. To start with, nothing changes in public. I'm the professor, you're the student."

I nod in understanding.

"And for the final exam, I'm going to have my teaching assistant proctor the exam. I'm going to assign random numbers to each student and grade anonymously. If anything ever gets out about us, nobody can say I favored you at all."

"Makes sense." I pause. "You've really thought about this."

"The whole trip here. My time with you is precious." Taking my hand, he holds it up to his face. "I don't want us to risk anything or have anything taint our future."

I blink, shocked by the tears that suddenly fall from my eyes. "Future?"

He meets my gaze, staring into my eyes. "I know it's fast. I know we have a lot to learn about each other, but that's what I want. The chance for a very real future."

"I want that, too."

"Good. Then let me do everything I can to protect it."

I nod. Because I've never wanted anything more.

✧   ✧   ✧

Shane

IS THERE REALLY such a thing as *the one*? Because I sure as hell am certain Amber is it for me.

The whole way home from the hospital, my focus wasn't on my sick father but his attitude towards Amber. I'll be damned if I'll tell her the rude things my father said. Instead I'll do everything in my power to get through the next two weeks and move on with our lives.

I drop her off at her house and walk her to her door, stepping inside.

"Can you stay?" she asks.

"I wish I could, but I think we need to just say goodbye." Before I can react, I step closer, easing her against the wall. "But don't think it isn't hard for me. Don't think I don't want you. I'm just trying to be smart." I've been weak the last two days, giving in to my need for her, but we need to walk a fine line from now on.

She strokes her hand down my cheek, her gaze soft on mine. "I understand. There will be plenty of time after class ends."

I brace a hand on the wall behind her, dip my head, and close my mouth over hers, devouring her, my entire body consumed with desire. My cock throbs against the rough denim of my jeans, and I rub myself against her. Moaning, she threads her fingers into my hair and holds me in place, rocking her hips against mine.

Dammit, I am too close to saying fuck it and taking her to bed. But if I do that, I won't want to leave in the morning. There will never be a good time to part ways, and eventually we'll get caught by someone and my worst nightmare will happen all over again.

With regret, I step back, leaving the warmth of her body, and she releases her hold.

"Go, Shane. Just leave now."

I nod, drawing in a rough breath. "Bye, beautiful. I'll talk to you soon."

She smiles, but I catch the sheen of frustrated tears. Forcing my heavy legs to move, I head out to my car and close myself inside. I lay my head on the steering wheel and groan. Doing the right thing shouldn't feel so damned wrong. I console myself with the fact that the next two weeks will pass slowly, but they *will* pass. And then nothing will stop us from being together.

CHAPTER SIX

Amber

WITH THE ECONOMICS final coming up, I increase my tutoring to twice a week. I don't want to risk failing and having to take the course all over again. In addition, I invite my study group over to my house for an extra session. I sense I'm not the only one struggling, and I think another couple of hours talking about the material will help.

I am grateful the other students don't hold my age against me as a reason not to include me. And though I have a wealth of life experience they don't, I enjoy their company.

They show up around seven, and I put out chips and soda. As usual, the girls come together. Tamara Acker, Bonnie Green, and Rhonda May arrive arguing over whether or not a guy I don't know is interested in Rhonda as something more than a friend. The guys, two of them, Dan Markham and Jeff Rhodes, come late. Also as usual.

The discussion about said guy's interest in Rhonda

continues even after the study group guys show up.

"What do you think, Amber? If a guy flirts, is he interested?" Rhonda, a pretty brunette, asks.

I crunch on a baked chip before answering. "Depends if he's a natural flirt with everyone. I'd have to know his personality before I could answer that."

"You see? And he is a flirt with most girls," Rhonda says to Bonnie and Tamara. "It's not just about me."

"Except the way he looks at you is different," Tamara argues.

"Agreed." This comes from Bonnie.

"So, two against one," I muse. I've never gone for the overtly flirtatious ones. Both Levi and Shane have that intense focus in common. Once they saw what they wanted, they just knew. They didn't need to flirt with the world.

Speaking of Shane, he hasn't disappeared on me. In the week since he dropped me off after the trip to the hospital to see his dad, he texted me nightly to talk and we really are getting to know each other a lot more. Not just superficial things like he prefers vanilla to chocolate, though he does, but that his mother lives twenty minutes away and he wants me to meet her before school starts again in September. He is neat, not fastidious; I like a clean house as well. And he is pretty good at sexting, as I've learned a day or two into our nightly *talks*.

"Amber? Where did you drift off to?" Dan asks.

I blush and shake my head. "Sorry. I was thinking about my son," I lie. "He was supposed to call earlier and didn't."

Dan frowns. "Well, we said we wanted to get started. Unless you're feeling like you don't need us now that your grades have gone up?"

I blink at his somewhat annoyed tone. Of everyone in the room, I like Dan the least. He has an attitude that rubs me the wrong way, and he definitely prefers when other people don't do well in class and he does.

"I'd hardly call C's a solid enough grade," I say, hating how defensive I sound. "Of course I need all of your help. I suggested this meeting, didn't I?"

"Shut up, Dan," Tamara says. "Amber has responsibilities you can't understand."

Now I feel bad about lying regarding my thoughts, but Dan didn't have to be such a jerk. Still, they've taken me into their group, making it worth putting up with his bullshit that includes bragging about how he is going into his father's financial firm after he gets his MBA. Like everyone, he has years of college and then business school to get through first.

The rest of the night passes without incident, and we part ways, but we'll see each other in class on Monday.

Seven more days until the final.

Seven more days until I can see Shane in public and act on my feelings.

I can handle a week.

After locking up for the night, I head for the bathroom, wash off my makeup, brush my teeth, and change into my favorite silk nightshirt.

I've just climbed into bed when my phone rings, and my body immediately responds, knowing it is Shane on the other end.

"Hi," I say on a breathy whisper.

"Hey, there. How was study group?" he asks.

"Productive." I don't like to mention the other students to him since they are in his class. No reason to let him know what an ass Dan is. He'll be out of my life soon enough.

"Are you in bed?" Shane asks, his voice low and gruff.

I shift on top of the covers. I haven't crawled underneath yet. "I am. How was your day?"

"Busy. Buried in research."

"And you love it," I say.

"I do."

I've come to realize he is most at home in his office at work or in the house he is renting, researching and getting lost in his economic theories ... that I despise, and that is putting it mildly. Good thing we have other things in common. We both love dogs but neither of us has time for a pet, at least right now, neither of us loves to cook but we both know how since we don't want to starve and I have another mouth to feed.

But I hate his taste in pizza toppings and we have to order half and half. Pepperoni makes me want to gag and he hates mushrooms. I can live with that, I think wryly.

I yawn, the sound coming out of my mouth before I can control it. "Excuse me," I say, laughing.

"Someone's tired."

I stretch out on my queen-size bed. "I had a long day studying, but I'm a little worked up with all those theories and things in my head. I don't know if I'll be able to fall asleep so fast."

"I have the solution for calming your mind." He chuckles, the sound low, deep, and sexy.

I squeeze my thighs together, knowing exactly what he has in mind. Sometimes he sends me sexy text messages, and other times he talks me through what he'd do to me if we were actually together.

"Yeah? Tell me more."

"Well, I know if I were there, I'd use my mouth to make you come before filling you deep with my cock. Seeing as how we have to wait for that, I'll just have to give you an orgasm another way. That'll take your mind off of math and theory and put it exactly where it belongs. On feeling good. On me."

"I can do that," I murmur.

"What are you wearing?" he asks.

"A silk nightshirt and underwear."

"Mmm-hmm. Okay, pull those sexy panties down your legs and expose that sweet pussy for me." His voice rumbles low in my ear.

Doing as he asks, I place the phone beside me, put him on speaker, then hook my fingers into my underwear and wriggle them down my thighs, pulling them completely off. They'll only be in the way.

"Done."

"You know what to do now, don't you?"

My breath hitches at his gruff voice, my finger automatically going to my clit. I am already wet with arousal, and I run my fingers through the moisture and moan aloud at the delicious waves rippling through me.

"Good girl. Do what you like best. What you're going to teach me next time we're alone together."

I begin to move my finger in circles, the tip sliding repetitively over my sensitive clit. Normally it would take me a long time to come if I was alone, but in the last week, with Shane instructing me, whispering naughty things in my ear, it isn't difficult at all.

"Shane," I say on a low groan.

"Keep going. Do you want to know what I'm doing?" he asks.

I close my eyes, unable to withstand the sensations and focus on anything around me. "Yes." I arch my hips and press down harder.

"I've got my hand around my cock, my eyes are shut, and I'm imagining you, working yourself until you come."

At the admission, I realize his breathing has picked up and taken on a rougher sound. He is obviously pumping himself with his hand, his body as primed and ready as mine is.

On that thought, I whimper and squeeze myself harder. Stars flicker behind my eyes and everything around me explodes in bright lights and wondrous sensation. "Shane!"

"I love that you scream my name when you come. God, yes. Fuck, Amber."

I hear the words, my name, and know he's reached his orgasm as well, and my body gives another little tremor before my legs fall to the mattress and I lay trying to catch my breath.

"Damn, if this is what you do to me over the phone, I can't imagine the next time we're together."

I can't help the smile that lifts my lips.

"Are you okay?"

"Yeah."

"Gonna sleep okay now?" His voice sounds raspy and so close, as if he was by my side. But his arms aren't around me, and I'm alone.

"I will, but I miss you." The words come naturally and without thought, making me realize I am in so deep with this man.

"I miss you, too. Another week."

"Seven days. We've got this," I say as much to myself as to him.

"And then we've got each other."

On that very pleasant thought, we say good night and I roll over, my body satisfied and my thoughts on Shane as I drift off to sleep.

✧　✧　✧

Amber

THE LAST ECONOMICS class falls on the day before the final exam. I didn't think I'd ever feel ready, but I know I've done all I can to get myself to the point where I can walk into that room with some confidence.

Shane is going over the more difficult concepts when I hear the low buzz of my cell phone in my bag. I forgot to shut it off before walking into the lecture hall, but he doesn't seem to notice.

A quick glance tells me it is Carrie, who rarely texts, so I peek at the message. *EVERYTHING IS OKAY but L.J. had a little accident. Five stitches in his leg. Wanted you to know but promise he's FINE.*

Panic and worry rush through me. I believe Carrie and trust her to take care of my son, and if something really serious happened, that text would have said to call her immediately. But to me, stitches are a big deal.

It means my boy's first trip to the emergency room, his first time getting sewn up, without his mom there. Worried and needing to talk to L.J., I gather my things and, without a glance around me, rush out of the room. Without waiting, I drop my things right outside the door and pull out my phone.

A second later, Carrie's face is on the screen. "He's fine, Amber. I promise you."

Tears fall from my eyes. "I believe you. It's just that I'm not there."

Carrie's expression is soft and understanding. "He was a champ."

"What happened?" I ask, leaning against the wall outside the classroom.

"He didn't listen and ran to give Samuel the pair of scissors. I'm sorry, honey. I feel terrible and responsible."

I shake my head. "No! It could have happened while I was there, too. I know he's in good hands. Can

I talk to him?"

"Samuel took him to the ice cream shop across the street from where we're staying Uptown. I really felt like we were intruding on Landon's privacy after so long."

I smile in understanding. "Would you have L.J. FaceTime me as soon as he gets back?"

"Of course. Are you ready for your exams?" Carrie asks.

"One down, a paper turned in, and one more to go." I don't mention that it is the hardest one. I don't want anyone to know how much I've struggled.

"Well, good luck and we'll talk soon. And don't worry."

Easier said than done, but I don't want Carrie to feel worse than she already does. We disconnect the call just as the class ends, and the students stream out of the lecture hall.

Realizing I took my backpack but left my small purse on the floor by my chair, I wait for everyone to leave and head back inside. I see my little bag on the floor and bend down to grab it.

When I rise, Shane is by my side. "Is everything okay? You bolted out of your seat and scared the shit out of me."

I manage a smile though I still feel shaky and am beyond upset. "I'd left my phone on by mistake. Carrie texted me. L.J. fell and needed stitches. She said he was fine but I needed to talk to her."

His gaze is one of complete understanding. "And? He's okay?"

I bite down on my lower lip, which has begun trembling. "He is. He was running with a pair of scissors." I shake my head and mutter, "Boys."

Shane raises a hand and slides his palm behind my neck. "Did you speak to him?"

"No. He went for ice cream with his grandfather."

Shane's low chuckle reassures me somewhat. "If he's up for ice cream, he must not be in too much pain. I'm sure they numbed the area first."

Tears begin to fall from my eyes unexpectedly, and Shane swears, then pulls me into his arms. "Shhh. He's fine. You're just upset because you weren't there for him."

"How did you know that?" I ask.

"Because I know you." He slides his fingers through my hair, and I let my emotions free, sniffling into his white dress shirt beneath his jacket. I like that he always dresses for class, taking even summer session oh so seriously. My professor, I muse, my thought taking me off guard.

Mine.

I want him to be mine, because in the short time I've known him, I've fallen in love with everything that is Shane Warden. But I'm not ready to tell him. Not while we are still in professor-student limbo.

"You okay now?" he asks.

I nod, wanting another minute in his safe, secure arms.

That is my mistake.

"I knew it." Dan stands by the last row of seats, his phone in his hand, aimed at us. "I knew you didn't raise your grades on your own."

"What the hell?" Shane, who has already separated himself from me, strides up the aisle toward the smug punk. "What are you doing?" he asks him.

"Proving what I suspected. That she fucked her way to a passing grade."

"But… No. I didn't! I had a tutor. I—"

Shane holds up a hand, cutting her off. "Don't bother arguing with him," he says in that authoritative voice I remember from the first day of class. "I'll deal with this. Amber, you can leave."

I blink but the tears fall anyway, the entire emotion of the last few minutes catching up with me … along with the fear that Dan's accusation could cost me everything.

✧　　✧　　✧

Amber

I PACE BACK and forth in my house. It is the not knowing how Shane is handling Dan that both concerns and frightens me. I came home from the incident shaken, but L.J. FaceTimed me almost as soon as I walked in the door, so I had no choice but to put on a bright smile and talk to my son.

Instead of expressing pain or being upset, L.J. was eager to show me his stitches. He had ice cream stains on his face, and he was chatty as ever, allowing me to breathe, at least about him. I duly lecture him about the dangers of running with scissors and not listening to his grandparents but figure he's been punished enough by the hospital experience. I have no doubt the stitches and numbing hurt him badly. I wince at the thought but force deep breaths into my lungs. He is fine.

Is Shane?

This is his worst nightmare, the one thing he went out of his way to avoid happening … and I caused it. I remained in his arms despite the risk. I let us get caught by someone who clearly has issues either with me or anyone he feels threatened by, though why he targeted me makes no sense.

I rub my hands over my arms and try to concentrate on studying for tomorrow's test while I wait to hear from Shane. It isn't easy … and he never calls.

He does return my text with a generic answer.

Don't worry. I have it handled. Will talk to you after the test. Good luck.

Handled how? Don't worry why? What is going on? The not knowing is killing me, but I understand he wants me to focus on the exam, and I need to do just that. Unfortunately I toss and turn all night.

The next morning, I drag myself to the test, tired, cranky, and concerned about how I'll handle the exam on little sleep and the worry clawing inside me.

Did he get in trouble and does he blame me? Is that why he is waiting to talk to me until after the test? I walk into the lecture hall expecting to see Shane. Although I know he wants the teaching assistant to proctor the exam, I thought he'd at least speak to the class first or wish us luck.

His absence makes it even more difficult to concentrate, but I know how much rides on my passing. Every higher-level class in business requires this entry-level course first. I want to set a positive example for L.J., want to prove to Landon, Jason, and Tanner that their faith in me is well placed. That lending me money for school wasn't a mistake.

Across the room, Dan glares at me, and I don't know what to make of his attitude. He has the upper hand, after all. He could report Shane to the dean and… no. I can't think about that now. Later. Later I'll see what happened.

Pushing every thought aside but economics, I draw a deep breath and settle in to work.

✧   ✧   ✧

Shane

I PACE THE hall outside the dean's office, waiting to be called in. Yesterday, after being caught by Dan, instead of letting the kid go and having yet another student make a mess of my life, I took control of the situation. I marched Dan and his damned cell phone and the recording of me holding Amber in my arms straight to the dean's office.

"Show him," I said to a shocked Dan. "Show Dean Frost what you have on your phone."

Sputtering and unsure what my end game was, Dan hit the play button and the video of Shane and Amber came up.

Dean Frost watched, an unhappy expression on his face, and my gut twisted hard.

"I see," the man said, then turned his gaze on Dan. "And why did you film this?"

"Because she obviously slept her way to a good grade! It's not fair. The rest of us have to work for what we get," Dan said, his cheeks red with anger and frustration.

The dean stared at him. "You do realize this isn't the first time you've come to me with accusations about a student cheating."

That was news to me. I had issues with Dan's unhappiness with bad grades, but I hadn't known others did, too.

"But … this time I have proof." Dan gestured to the phone on the dean's desk.

"That remains to be seen." The older man folded his hands across his chest as he stared Dan down. "You, however, have issues with everyone but yourself. After the last time you accused Jeanne Clark of cheating, which she hadn't done—there were cameras in the classroom—I kept an eye on grades. You're struggling, young man. And you blame everyone but yourself. One more incident and I'll have no choice but to expel you. You can't go on accusing others with no consequences."

Fury lit Dan's features, and he stormed out of the room.

The dean then turned his gaze to me. "I know the boy's father. I suppose it's time we have a talk," he said on a sigh. "As for you, would you care to explain?" He gestured to the phone, which remained on his desk.

I blew out a long breath, gathering my thoughts. The dean knew my history and he understood this video looked bad. But I hadn't broken any school rules. And I covered myself regarding the test and grades.

I went on to explain that Amber had a frightening situation with her son and I'd merely been comforting her. However, I admitted to having a relationship with her. One that I put on hold until class was over. I gave the dean the name of Amber's tutor and asked the man to talk to the woman and find out how long she'd been working with Amber. Then I listed everything I did to keep the final exam fair and impartial.

"I can understand why you'd be careful, given your history," the man said. "What exactly is going on with you and this student?"

"Woman," I corrected him. "She's a full-grown adult who decided to go back to school."

"Aah. I hadn't realized."

I nodded. "But you need to know I intend to pursue a serious relationship with her now that class is over. And if you have a problem with that, if I need to choose between my job and Amber…" My heart nearly beat out of my chest as I drew a deep breath.

I'd been up most of the night contemplating this conversation and what was more important to me. And no matter how much I want tenure, no matter that I knew if I blew it at another school, my fault or not, I wouldn't get a third chance, I came to the same conclusion.

"I choose Amber."

The man's expression was bland, his eyes not giving away a damned thing as he said, "I'd like the night to consider the situation."

So I went home alone. Not wanting Amber to worry about the fact that a decision would be made about my career, I didn't call her. If I spoke to her, I don't trust myself not to tell her everything, and she needs to focus on passing the test. So I texted her back, told her everything would be okay, and left the details until today.

Right now she is taking the exam.

And I am awaiting my fate.

"I was up much of the night," Dean Frost says.

Join the club, I think.

"As you know, you haven't broken school rules, but I do have to look at the ethical considerations of you dating a student."

"A former student of mine as of yesterday," I feel compelled to remind the older man.

Dean Frost nods. "Yes. And she is an adult, as you said. Although there is the argument to be made that any of our students over eighteen are adults. I'd be setting precedent."

I think I'm going to throw up. My career, everything I've worked for, is about to disappear before my eyes.

"However, the fact that she is not a young woman but an adult with experience behind her does help your cause. As does the fact that you stepped aside while class was going on. You covered the exams, made them impartial, and handled things with impartiality."

His hard stare doesn't allow me to read his final thoughts at all. I stand, hands clenched, shoulders tense, and wait.

With a frown, the dean says, "I can't say I like it or that it's going to make things easy on us going forward ... but you would also have a case against us for unlawful termination if I fired you. Which I don't want to do. You're a good professor. A solid addition to the faculty. And you got a raw deal twice, first at your last school and now again here. I knew Dan was a loose cannon, and I did nothing to prevent him from causing trouble again."

"So where does this leave us?" I ask.

Dean Frost extends his hand. "It leaves you with your position intact, Professor Warden."

"Thank you, sir." Relief filling me, I clasp the other man's hand. "I appreciate your understanding."

To my surprise, Dean Frost smiles, dropping the stern formality he held on to throughout our meeting. "I met my wife when I was eighteen. It was love at first sight. I'm not going to deny you what's obviously true love."

I grin. Although I didn't say the words to myself, I know it's true. Why else would I be willing to give up my job for Amber?

"So what are you waiting for?" Dean Frost asks. "Go get your girl."

CHAPTER SEVEN

Amber

I FINISH MY exam, too afraid to hope. Yes, I think I passed. But did I get a C? C-? D? It is anybody's guess. I need the D to pass the class, and I really believe in my heart it is possible. But even with that huge concern off my shoulders, I'm not free of worry because I still don't know what Shane's *Don't worry, I have it handled* text meant.

I step into the bright sunshine and look around. If I hoped to see Shane, I am disappointed. There are plenty of happy students whose final test of the summer has ended but no Shane.

I make my way home, taking the long way, needing to walk and clear my head. L.J. is coming home tomorrow with his grandparents, and real life is about to descend on me. I am so excited to see my baby, but I know it means more responsibilities, more routine, more schedules. I'll have to find ways to find time to see Shane ... if he still wants to see me after what went down with Dan.

By the time I arrive on my street, I decide I'm going to Shane's house to talk to him and find out what is going on. Except I don't need to.

Shane sits on my doorstep, waiting for me.

With trepidation, I meet him at the bottom of the porch.

"Hi."

"Hi. How was your test?"

"You're a hard teacher, Professor Warden. But I think, I hope I passed."

A pleased smile lifts his sexy lips. "I asked Eric to grade them this afternoon," he says of the teacher's assistant. "They should be posted by morning."

I blow out a deep breath. "Good. Another night tossing and turning." I smile wryly. "Don't worry, I expected to have to wait to find out."

I pull my purse in front of me and look for my keys, extracting them from my bag. "Want to come inside?" My heart pounds in my chest, the fear of not knowing what is going on consuming me.

"Sure." He smiles at me, but I still don't know where we stand.

After letting us into the house, I close the door behind us and turn to face him. "I can't take it anymore. What happened with Dan?"

"I took him to Dean Frost myself and showed him the video. Dan has a history of reporting people for cheating when he doesn't do as well as he'd like in a class. The dean wasn't pleased with him. I don't think he's going to be my problem anymore. As for us…"

"Oh, my God. Is he angry? Am I in trouble? Are you?"

He shakes his head and tries to breathe deeply and evenly.

"Then what did he say?"

Shane's serious expression makes my stomach twist with uncertainty.

"At first he asked for the night to think, which was why I didn't want to explain things last night. I didn't want to leave you hanging the night before a test. Well, any more than you already were." He shakes his head, a wry twist to his lips.

I twist my hands in front of me, nerves getting the best of me. "And this morning? What did he say?"

"Before I tell you what he said, you need to know what I said. In no uncertain terms, I told him that if it came down to a choice between my job and you, I chose you."

"You did *what?*" I get light-headed. "I need to sit down."

Chuckling, he wraps an arm around my waist and leads me to the nearest sofa in the family room, easing me onto a cushion and sitting beside me.

He clasps my hand in his. "I'm serious. I know it's

early days, but I know what I'm feeling for you and it's not casual. It's not something I'm going to walk away from."

"But your job, your career … tenure."

"I'd have dealt with losing it if I had to… Luckily I don't have to. Dean Frost is a smart man. He was able to discern the differences between us and me and an eighteen- or nineteen-year-old student. And regardless, I didn't violate any school rules or policy. Although I have a feeling that might change going forward, but it won't affect us." His hands tighten around mine.

I swallow hard, trying to come to terms with what he's done. "You risked your career … for me."

Meeting my gaze, his expression softens. "For us. I risked being terminated for *us* because I believe what we could have is too special to let go."

My heart thuds in my chest. "I think so, too," I whisper, almost afraid to jinx what we share.

"So we're in agreement? We're together?" He moves closer, as if my answer is a foregone conclusion. Which, of course, it is.

"Yes!"

He rises, pulling me to my feet.

Happy tears in my eyes, I grin, take a few steps, and jump into his arms, wrapping my legs around his waist and trusting he'll catch me. Then I press my lips to his.

I kiss him, and all my worries flee, replaced with hopes and dreams I thought I gave up on. After the kiss, which is long and beautiful, I draw back.

"L.J. is coming home tomorrow," I tell him. Although he is saying all the right words, I feel compelled to remind him of my real life. The one he hasn't experienced yet.

He meets my gaze, all the while holding me tight. "And I can't wait to meet him."

"Really?"

He tilts his head to the side. "Really. Haven't I done everything possible to prove that to you?"

I nod. "You really have. Now can we go to bed and let me prove to you how much I appreciate you?"

He strides out of the family room, down the hall, and into my room. Laughing, he tosses me down on the bed and strips me out of my clothes. I do the same to him, and we come together, skin to skin.

Pressing my check against his, I close my eyes and breathe in deep, feeling his chest rise and fall beneath mine.

"I love you," I say, the words tumbling out. "I mean—"

"I love you, too, so you'd better not mean anything else."

I let out a puff of air. "Well, no. I don't. I just thought maybe it was too soon or I shouldn't have said it yet…"

"It's soon. I get that, but if we feel it, what's wrong with saying it?" He slides his lips over mine, and his thick erection pulses against my belly.

At the feel of him hard against me, my legs open and his cock comes to rest at my entrance. "Amber." He lets out a groan.

"I'm on birth control for other reasons. And you know I haven't been with anyone in a long time. I've had an annual exam and I'm clean. I want to feel you bare inside me."

He visibly swallows hard. "I wouldn't put you at risk. I'm fine, too."

His cock seems to throb in response and I grin. "Then what are you waiting for?"

He slides into me and everything inside me settles. My world seems brighter. Everything that is uncertain falls into place.

Long after I climax and he comes right along with me, I lie in his arms, happy and complete.

✧　　✧　　✧

Shane

THE NEXT MORNING, after a breakfast of scrambled eggs and bacon, made by Amber and me together, I am dressing after a shower, stuck in my clothes from the day before. My gaze falls on a long tube leaning against the wall.

Amber strides out of the bathroom, makeup complete, dressed for the day in a pair of jeans and a tank top, looking fresh and sexy.

"What are your plans for the day?" she asks me.

"I was going to go home and change. Then I hoped to come back and meet L.J.?" I hear the hope in my voice. But how can we become closer, more like a family, if I don't first meet and spend time with her son?

"Sounds good! I want you two to meet." She braces her hands on my shoulders, leans down, and kisses me.

"Hey, what's that?" I point to the rolled tube I noticed earlier.

She grins. "A Spiderman Fathead. L.J. wanted a life-size superhero on his wall. I thought I'd surprise him when he came home, but I didn't anticipate how big it actually was. I can't put it up by myself."

"Then let's do it. He's going to be home soon, right? So let's hurry and put it up."

Her eyes light at the idea.

For the next thirty minutes, we struggle getting the life-size decal onto the wall behind the head of the bed, but between the two of us, we manage.

"You do realize it's going to have to come down when I paint the room blue?" she asks, a little out of breath from our work.

I groan. "We'll deal with that when the time comes—"

The sound of the doorbell cuts me off.

"Who could that be? It's too early for L.J. They said they were leaving around eleven and would be home by lunch." She heads for the front door and I follow.

Amber peeks through the side narrow window and lets out a shriek of excitement, unlocking the deadbolt and yanking the door open.

"Baby!" She kneels down and pulls a brown-haired boy into her arms.

He hugs her back but very quickly begins squirming to escape her hold.

"I think you'd better let him go," a muscular dark-haired man with a scruff of beard says from behind him.

I know immediately from photos I've seen this is L.J.'s father's twin. His Uncle Landon.

Amber releases her hold, but her gaze never leaves her son. "You'd better believe I expect more hugs later."

"Mooom!" He groans her name. "I have to go to the bathroom!" he says and takes off at a run.

I chuckle, drawing the other man's attention to me. "Who are you?"

"Landon, don't be rude!" Amber holds up a hand against his chest. "Landon Bennett, this is Shane Warden. Shane, this is L.J.'s uncle," Amber says, eyeing the man warily.

I extend my hand, and Landon takes it, shaking hard.

Okay, I get it. The man is protective of Amber and L.J. Well, he damn well better learn he comes second to me now. "Nice to meet you."

"It's early for you to be here," Landon says pointedly.

"And you're ridiculous! I'm a grown woman. You have no say in what I do. Although in this case I better warn you, you're going to be seeing a lot of Shane, so I'd appreciate it if you got to know him and didn't just act like an ass on first meeting."

"Mom! Five bucks in the swear jar," L.J. says, rejoining us.

She sighs. "I unpacked it, and it's in the kitchen. You can watch me add money later." She ruffles his hair. "I swear you grew a couple of inches. We need to set up a measuring wall here."

Landon grins. "He's certainly eaten enough to have a growth spurt. Which reminds me, we stopped for breakfast on the road."

Clearly the reprimand has been forgotten. I don't need Amber fighting my battles for me. I can win L.J.'s uncles over on my own, but I appreciate her coming to my defense.

"Why did you leave so early?" she asks.

"Your boy couldn't wait to see you." Landon chuckles.

"L.J., why don't you take your suitcase into your room?" She gestures to the bag with wheels that Landon placed inside the door.

"Okay." He pulls the luggage along, and as we watch him go, she meets my gaze with a knowing grin.

"Cool! Mom, you got me the Fathead!"

She laughs. "I'm going to talk to him for a few minutes. Can you behave while I'm gone?" she asks Landon, who is still eyeing me warily.

"Go ahead, we'll be fine," I assure her. I want a word with the other man.

I wait until Amber disappears, deliberately not watching her sexy ass, before I turn to Landon. "I get it," I say before the other man can speak. "You're protective. You're worried. You don't know me, don't trust me, and you don't live nearby."

The other man cocks his head to one side. "That about sums it up."

I hold up my hands. "I love her, and she loves me."

Landon lets out a snort. "In one short summer?"

I ignore him. I heard from Amber how quickly Landon fell for Vivi. The man has no room to judge us. "In the meantime, I'd appreciate it if you cut me some slack. Get to know me before deciding how you feel about me. And know I'd cut off my arm before I'd hurt them."

Arms folded across his chest, Landon studies me, his expression shifting a bit at my last comment. "You said them. So you understand they're a package deal. L.J. isn't some kid you can push aside so you can fuck his mom."

My blood boils at the careless words. "One," I say through clenched teeth, "don't talk about Amber like that. She's worth a lot more than a fuck," I mutter. "And two, it pisses me off you'd jump to that conclusion. I know L.J. is her world. I only want to be part of them. Not come between them."

Landon scrubs a hand over his face. "Fine. You pass. But I'll be watching you. Jason, Tanner, and I will all be keeping an eye out. Just because we're in New York doesn't mean we're not involved in their lives."

"I'd expect nothing less," I say. "I'm glad she had the three of you all these years."

"We're not going anywhere."

I shake my head and let out a low chuckle. "I didn't think you were."

"Everything okay in here?" Amber asks, returning from L.J.'s room.

"Perfect." I wrap an arm around her waist and kiss her cheek.

"Good. Landon, are you staying for the day?" she asks.

He shakes his head. "The club needs me. I just offered to take the ride so Mom and Dad could go straight home. They said they'll call you later so you can work out a schedule for when school starts."

She shoots him a grateful look. "Thanks for everything." She hugs him and he returns the gesture, but even I can see it is all platonic … even if he does look exactly like his twin brother had.

I let out a relieved breath I wasn't aware of holding.

A few seconds later, Landon says his goodbyes and walks out to his car. Amber shuts the door to the house.

"Where's L.J.?" I ask.

"Doing his best to unpack. There are no dirty clothes, thank you, Carrie," Amber says with a grateful smile.

"Want me to go so you can spend some time alone?" I offer.

She wraps her arms around my waist and shakes her head. "I'd like my two boys to get to know each other. Unless you want to go home and change?"

I chuckle. "It can wait."

She stares up at me with those big, beautiful blue eyes. "We're a lot to handle," she says nervously.

"I can't wait to do it. I know the juggling of schedules won't be easy, finding time alone won't be simple, but I know what I'm getting into. And I'm all in."

She reaches onto her tiptoes and brushes her lips over mine. "I'm so glad. You changed my life, Shane Warden."

"Same, Amber Davis. And I couldn't be happier."

EPILOGUE

Shane

IT IS A day to celebrate. Amber received her combined bachelor of arts degree—with her minor in business—and her master's in education, and I earned tenure at the end of this school year. At the New York uncles' insistence, we all came to Manhattan for a celebration at the nightclub, which they opened on a Sunday afternoon just for this special occasion.

With my arm around Amber and L.J., now a lanky teenager beside us, I walk into Club TEN29, aptly named after the date Levi Bennett passed away. But the club is now a happy place, one where people come to have fun and celebrate. The owners, L.J.'s uncles, have all come around and accepted my presence in Amber's and L.J.'s lives. We moved in together when my lease ran out, and since we were always at Amber's anyway, we decided to live together then.

Although I was ready for more, I knew Amber wanted to finish school. She likes to put all her focus on one big thing at a time, and a wedding would have thrown her off her studying game, no matter how small we might have made it. And with the guys finding their wives, the size of our pseudo-family has expanded.

The party is small, just close family and friends. Amber's parents flew up from Florida, for which I am grateful as their presence plays into my plans. I wait until the end of the day, after presents are opened and a lot of food eaten.

Even my father and stepmother are here, something my mom has no problem accepting. Many years have passed, and she is long over their marriage and years together. In the time since his heart attack, my dad made an attempt to be part of my life and I've reciprocated warily. Now things are decent between us all.

Amber, wearing a pretty pink dress and gold heels, stands by my side. Knowing there is no time like the present, I clear my throat. "Excuse me," I say. "I'd like to say something."

The murmurs and conversation quiet down and all eyes are on me. I slide a hand into my suit jacket, which I wore because the party was dressy and I wanted this day to be special and one to remember.

Amber turns to me, questions in her wide blue eyes.

"First I want to thank the guys, Landon, Jason, and

Tanner, for the fabulous party, and Faith, Scarlett and Vivi for helping."

A small round of clapping follows.

"I also want to thank them for giving a college professor a chance with this woman here. I know if they'd put their foot down, it could have made Amber's choices much more difficult." In the years since that awkward meeting with Landon at Amber's front door, we've all become good friends.

"I can make my own decisions, you know," she says beside me.

I nod. "I also know you would not have wanted to argue with your family. I'm glad they didn't make you." I tip my head at the three men who stand with their hands around the respective women in their lives.

"Thank you, Carrie and Samuel, for treating me like I'm part of the family. It means the world to me."

The couple smiles at me.

"Thanks to Lydia and John for raising such a fabulous woman and to my mom for being my rock."

She brings her hands to her heart and blows me a kiss.

"Finally, L.J., thanks for sharing your mom with me. And thank you for giving me permission to do this." I reach into my pocket and pull out the ring I bought a long time ago. I've just been waiting for Amber to be ready. Then I drop to one knee.

Amber gasps. I know she expected a graduation and congratulations party … not this.

"Amber, from the second you bumped into me on campus—"

"Umm, I think you bumped into me," she says with a grin.

"From the second we bumped into each other and I looked into your eyes, I think I recognized the other half of my soul. I just wasn't ready to admit to myself I was ready. We all know it didn't take long for me to fall for your laughter, your warmth, and your poor, poor economics skills."

The tinkling of laughter warms me inside.

"I fell for your son the minute he smiled at me. And we became a family. Now I just want to make it legal and tie you to me forever. Amber, will you marry me?" I hold out the round diamond with pavé stones surrounding it.

"Yes! A million times, yes."

I slide the ring onto her hand and then her lips are on mine. We kiss too briefly and then I stand up, grinning like a fool, Amber pulled tightly against me.

I barely hear the clapping around us. All I can focus on is the woman in my arms. The boy beaming with approval beside us. The family that is now mine.

Thanks for reading The Sexy Series!

Continue with the Dare family in **Falling for Trouble**, book 1 in The Dare to Fall Series.

Start reading The Kingston Family with **Just One Night**.

Want even more Carly books?

CARLY'S BOOKLIST by Series – visit:
https://www.carlyphillips.com/CPBooklist

Sign up for Carly's Newsletter:
https://www.carlyphillips.com/CPNewsletter

Join Carly Phillips' Readers Lounge on Facebook:
https://www.carlyphillips.com/CarlysCorner

Carly on Facebook:
https://www.carlyphillips.com/CPFanpage

Carly on Instagram:
https://www.carlyphillips.com/CPInstagram

Carly's Booklist

newest series listed first

The Dare to Fall Series

Book 1: Falling for Trouble (Rainey Dare & Lucas Carras)

Book 2: Falling for Real (Kaylee Martin & Tristan Hayes)

Book 3: Falling for Love (Sophie Monroe & Jack Dare)

The Sterling Family

Book 1: Just One More Moment (Remington Sterling & Raven Walsh)

Book 2: Just One More Dare (Dex Kingston & Samantha Dare)

Book 3: Just One More Mistletoe (Max Corbin & Brandy Bloom)

Book 4: Just One More Temptation (Fallon Sterling & Noah Powers)

Book 5: Just One More Affair (Jared Sterling & Charlotte Kendall)

Book 6: Just One More Time (Aiden Sterling & Brooke Snyder)

Book 7: Just One More Date (Leo Watson & Camille Hendricks)

The Dirty Dares
Book 1: Just One Dare (Aurora Kingston &
Nick Dare)
Book 2: Just One Kiss (Jade Dare & Knox Sinclair)
Book 3: Just One Taste (Asher Dare &
Nicolette Bettencourt)
Book 4: Just One Fling (Harrison Dare &
Winter Capwell)
Book 5: Just One Tease (Zach Dare &
Hadley Stevens)
Novella: Just One Summer (Maddox James &
Gabriella Davenport)

The Kingston Family
Book 1: Just One Night (Linc Kingston &
Jordan Greene)
Book 2: Just One Scandal (Chloe Kingston &
Beck Daniels)
Book 3: Just One Chance (Xander Kingston &
Sasha Keaton)
Book 4: Just One Spark (Dash Kingston &
Cassidy Forrester)
Just Another Spark – Short Story (Dash &
Cassidy revisited)
Novella: Just One Wish (Axel Forrester &
Tara Stillman)

Dare Nation

Book 1: Dare to Resist (Austin Prescott &
Quinn Stone)

Book 2: Dare to Tempt (Damon Prescott &
Evie Wolfe)

Book 3: Dare to Play (Jaxon Prescott & Macy Walker)

Book 4: Dare to Stay (Brandon Prescott &
Willow James)

Novella: Dare to Tease (Hudson Northfield &
Brianne Prescott)

The Sexy Series

Book 1: More Than Sexy (Jason Dare &
Faith Lancaster)

Book 2: Twice As Sexy (Tanner Grayson &
Scarlett Davis)

Book 3: Better Than Sexy (Landon Bennett &
Vivienne Clark)

Novella: Always Sexy (Shane Warden & Amber Davis)

The Knight Brothers

Book 1: Take Me Again (Sebastian Knight &
Ashley Easton)

Novella: Take The Bride (Sierra Knight &
Ryder Hammond)

Book 2: Take Me Down (Parker Knight &
Emily Stevens)

Book 3: Dare Me Tonight (Ethan Knight &
Sienna Dare)
Take Me Now – Short Story (Harper Stevens &
Matt Banks)

The New York Dares
Book 1: Dare to Surrender (Gabe Dare &
Isabelle Masters)
Book 2: Dare to Submit (Decklan Dare &
Amanda Collins)
Book 3: Dare to Seduce (Max Savage & Lucy Dare)

Dare to Love Series
Book 1: Dare to Love (Ian Dare & Riley Taylor)
Book 2: Dare to Desire (Alex Dare & Madison Evans)
Book 3: Dare to Touch (Dylan Rhodes & Olivia Dare)
Book 4: Dare to Hold (Scott Dare & Meg Thompson)
Book 5: Dare to Rock (Avery Dare & Grey Kingston)
Book 6: Dare to Take (Tyler Dare & Ella Shaw)
A Very Dare Christmas – Short Story (Ian &
Riley revisited)

Billionaire Bad Boys
Book 1: Going Down Easy (Kaden Barnes &
Lexie Parker)
Book 2: Going Down Fast (Lucas Monroe &
Maxie Sullivan)

Book 3: Going Down Hard (Derek West &
Cassie Storms)
Book 4: Going In Deep (Julian Dane &
Kendall Parker)
Going Down Again – Short Story (Kade &
Lexie revisited)

Bodyguard Bad Boys
Book 1: Rock Me (Ben Hollander &
Summer Michelle)
Book 2: Tempt Me (Austin Rhodes & Mia Atwood)
Novella: His To Protect (Talia Shaw & Shane Landon)

Serendipity Series
Book 1: Serendipity (Ethan Barron &
Faith Harrington)
Book 2: Kismet (Lissa Gardelli & Trevor Dane)
Book 3: Destiny (Nash Barron & Kelly Moss)
Book 4: Fated (Kate Andrews & Nick Mancini)
Book 5: Karma (Dare Barron & Liza McKnight)

Serendipity's Finest
Book 1: Perfect Fit (Michael Marsden & Cara Hartley)
Book 2: Perfect Fling (Erin Marsden & Cole Sanders)
Book 3: Perfect Together (Sam Marsden &
Nicole Farnsworth)
Book 4: Perfect Strangers (Alexa Collins &
Luke Thompson)

Hot Heroes Series

Book 1: Touch You Now (Halley Ward & Kane Harmon)

Book 2: Hold You Now (Phoebe Ward & Jake Nichols)

Book 3: Need You Now (Juliette Collins & Braden Clark)

Book 4: Want You Now (Andi Harmon & Kyle Davenport)

The Chandler Brothers

Book 1: The Bachelor (Roman Chandler & Charlotte Bronson)

Book 2: The Playboy (Rick Chandler & Kendall Sutton)

Book 3: The Heartbreaker (Chase Chandler & Sloane Carlisle)

The Lucky Series

Book 1: Lucky Charm (Derek Corwin & Gabrielle Donovan)

Book 2: Lucky Streak (Mike Corwin & Amber Rose Brennan)

Book 3: Lucky Break (Jason Corwin & Lauren Perkins)

Costas Sisters
Book 1: Under the Boardwalk (Ariana Costas &
Quinn Donovan)
Book 2: Summer of Love (Zoe Costas &
Ryan Baldwin)

Ty and Hunter
Book 1: Cross My Heart (Lilly Dumont & Ty Benson)
Book 2: Sealed with a Kiss (Molly Gifford &
Daniel Hunter)

The Hot Zone
Book 1: Hot Stuff (Annabelle Jordan &
Brandon Vaughn)
Book 2: Hot Number (Micki Jordan & Damian Fuller)
Book 3: Hot Item (Sophie Jordan & Riley Nash)
Book 4: Hot Property (Amy Stone & John Roper)

The Simply Series
Book 1: Simply Sinful (Kayla Luck &
Kane McDermott)
Book 2: Simply Scandalous (Catherine Luck &
Logan Montgomery)
Book 3: Simply Sensual (Ben Callahan &
Grace Montgomery)
Book 4: Body Heat (Jake Lowell & Brianne Nelson)
Book 5: Simply Sexy (Rina Lowell & Colin Lyons)

The Most Eligible Bachelor Series
Book 1: Kiss Me if You Can (Sam Cooper &
Lexie Davis)
Book 2: Love Me If You Dare (Rafe Mancuso &
Sara Rios)

Carly Classics
Book 1: The Right Choice (Carly Wexler &
Mike Novak)
Book 2: Perfect Partners (Chelsie Russell &
Griffin Stuart)
Book 3: Unexpected Chances (Dylan North &
Holly Evans)
Book 4: Worthy of Love (Kevin Manning &
Nikki Welles)

About the Author

Carly Phillips is the *NY Times*, *Wall Street Journal*, and *USA Today* bestselling author of over eighty sexy contemporary romances featuring hot men, strong women, and the emotionally compelling stories her readers have come to expect and love. She is happily married to her college sweetheart and lives outside New York City. She is the mother of two adult daughters and a Havanese puppy who stars on her social media and newsletter. Visit her website: www.carly phillips.com.